DONNA JO NAPOLI

HUSH

AN IRISH PRINCESS' TALE

ATHENEUM BOOKS FOR YOUNG READERS
NEW YORK   LONDON   TORONTO   SYDNEY

for Patrick Hill

✦   ✦   ✦

Atheneum Books for Young Readers
An imprint of Simon & Schuster Children's Publishing Division
1230 Avenue of the Americas, New York, New York 10020
This book is a work of fiction. Any references to historical
events, real people, or real locales are used fictitiously. Other names,
characters, places, and incidents are products of the author's
imagination, and any resemblance to actual events or locales
or persons, living or dead, is entirely coincidental.
Copyright © 2007 by Donna Jo Napoli
Map of Europe by Elena Furrow
All rights reserved, including the right of
reproduction in whole or in part in any form.
Book design by Michael McCartney
The text for this book is set in Adobe Jenson.
Manufactured in the United States of America
First Edition
2 4 6 8 10 9 7 5 3 1
Library of Congress Cataloging-in-Publication Data
Napoli, Donna Jo, 1948–
Hush : an Irish princess' tale / Donna Jo Napoli. — 1st ed.
p.   cm.
Summary: Fifteen-year-old Melkorka, an Irish princess, is
kidnapped by Russian slave traders and not only learns how to survive but
to challenge some of the brutality of her captors, who are fascinated by
her apparent muteness and the possibility that she is enchanted.
ISBN-13: 978-0-689-86176-5 • ISBN-10: 0-689-86176-1
[1. Slavery—Fiction. 2. Mutism, elective—Fiction. 3. Seafaring life—Fiction.
4. Princesses—Fiction. 5. Conduct of life—Fiction. 6. Middle Ages—Fiction.
7. Ireland—History—To 1172—Fiction.] I. Title.
PZ7.N15Hus 2007 • [Fic]-dc22 • 2007002676

```
*******************************
   New Hanover County Library
01/27/2020 6:54:22      910-798-6302
        PM
*******************************
 Automated Telephone Renewals
        910-798-6320
 Renew Online at
 http://www.nhclibrary.org
*******************************


Title:        Sock innovation :
Author:
A., Cookie. (DLC)n 2008069658
Item ID:      34200010659684
Due:          02/18/2020


Title:
Country weekend socks :
Author:
Weston, Madeline, author. (DLC)n
85360006
Item ID:      34200011037138
Due:          02/18/2020


Title:        Hush :
Author:
Napoli, Donna Jo, 1948- author.
(DLC)n 79085705
Item ID:      34200008438125
Due:          02/18/2020


Fine Balance for $9.20
This Account

*******************************
```

ACKNOWLEDGMENTS

Thanks to Eva, Robert, and Barry Furrow, Sascha Agran,
Stefan Brink, Anna Cohen, Neil Cavanaugh, Eric Eisenberg,
Maeve Hannon, Sheila Hannon, David Harrison, Patrick Hill,
Nick Kane, Samara Leist, Michael McCartney, Moses Nakamura,
Helen North, Ginee Seo, Valerie Shea, Richard Tchen, and Alison Velea.
Thanks go to the National Museum of Ireland in Dublin
and to the Trinity College Library at Dublin,
as well as to the librarians at Swarthmore College who helped me
collect the materials for researching this time and place.
And a special and multiple thank-you to my indefatigable
and ever-encouraging editor, Jordan Brown.

NOTE TO THE READER

In the Old Norse language spoken in the 900s
the letter Þ / þ is pronounced like the *th* in *think*.
The letter Ð / ð is pronounced like the *th* in *though*.
The letter Æ / æ is pronounced like the *a* in *cat*.

PART ONE

CHAPTER ONE:
THE BROOCH

"Mel, hurry up!" Brigid calls, splashing through puddles, heedless of the mud that has come up through the wooden-plank paving of the road. She is eight, which accounts for much of her bad behavior, but not all. "Please, Mel." She takes my hand and hangs on it, like she did when she was smaller. "There's so much to see in Dublin."

"And what will it be worth if Mother scolds you afterward for mud on the hem of your tunic and cloak?"

"A scolding is small price for such pleasure."

"Oh, Brigid, that's a new cloak, and it's beautiful." Indeed, the woad herb makes wool a stunning blue. I point. "Look, the fringes on the border are already mucked up."

"Well, then, it's too late, isn't it? I might as well run now. Besides, Mel, this is the first time we've been here. And we wouldn't even have come now if you hadn't begged Father. And Father wouldn't have agreed if it wasn't your birthday." She's out of breath from fast talk, but glowing with the logic of it. Mother always says Brigid can outreason us all. "And after so long squished in the chariot. And the smelly lodgings in the Kingdom of Meath midway. And then more bumpy time before dawn today. All that to get here. With the cursèd rain the whole way. Well, we're free now, and the sun is shining and we should play."

I can't help but agree, though her remarks about cursèd rain call for a response. "Rainfall is Eire land's most important blessing, Brigid." I tuck her hand over my arm as we walk. "We may not have much farming land, but we've got rivers and lakes, which make good fishing and good trading."

"Don't quote Father to me."

"You had better learn to quote him to yourself, then. And until you do, you had better listen to me."

"You're boring to listen to. Nuada is far better."

Nuada is our brother. He's thirteen—two years younger than me—but when the three of us get together for storytelling, it's Nuada who speaks. His voice is so sweet, cows give more milk when he sings. I've seen it.

"Be that as it may, you can't run through the mud." My voice scolds. "Someone will treat you poorly. You look like a wild child instead of a princess."

"Ah, that's it!" She laughs. "You want men to stare at you in your new cloak. You don't care about what I look like for myself."

"Don't be absurd. This is a Norse town. I don't care what the Norsemen think of me." I put my hand on top of hers and squeeze harder than I should. "You know very well I will marry Irish royalty from a kingdom much closer to our own Downpatrick."

"Then don't you worry about anyone treating me poorly. If they dare to, I'll shout who I am. No one bothers princesses. No one, no one. Not even Norsemen who have gone crazy . . . the ones they call Vikings." As she says that last word, she yanks herself free and jumps in front of me. Her hands become claws, her lips curl back from her teeth, her brow furrows, her nose wrinkles, her eyes squint fiercely.

That's the monster face Nuada makes when he tells us stories of Viking raids. I can't help but flinch. Vikings are no joking matter.

Brigid laughs and spins on her heel. She races ahead again. And with an excited cry of "Arrah!" she now turns a corner, out of sight.

I look around. No one seems to have paid attention to our little fight except two women slaves carrying raw wool in big baskets, and they hardly matter. When I give them a reproving glance, they quickly look down and duck into the spinner's shop.

I smooth my cloak. Brigid's right: I do love it. Red,

from madder, with a plaited border. My tunic is new too. Linen, spun from flax, not ordinary nettle. My maid-servant Delaney dyed it yellow from the weld plant.

Father gasped when I first put it on. He says colors play tricks. He fears them. But women know how to control the tricks. Mother's teaching me. That's why I picked the weld myself rather than sending a slave boy to the field. And that's why I urinated on my new tunic myself. My own urine not only holds the color fast, but ensures that the spirit in the color obeys me.

Brigid doesn't obey me, though, but she won't go far. The first new thing she sees will stop her. New things fascinate her.

And practically everything about this heathen town is new, which is why I begged Father to take me here for my birthday. Our small town bores me. The Kingdom of Downpatrick has only three thousand people, including those in the surrounding hills and valleys. And that's even counting slaves. But Dublin has that many living within the town walls, and the stench from their cooking and smoke and dampness pervades every shop-lined street. So many shops. Leather workers, shoemakers, bone workers, comb makers, every kind of craftsman and tradesman work within three spades of one another.

It amazes even Mother. She didn't want to come at first, her fear of Vikings is so strong. But once she saw the stores, she bustled about with a smile. She ordered gloves for Father, and she's now back at the toolmaker's, ordering a set of iron knives.

I'm going to buy something too. My new cloak needs the perfect brooch to secure it at the breast. Silver would stand out against red better than bronze or iron. I duck into the silversmith's.

He greets me with words I don't understand. Norse, undoubtedly. I stiffen a little. Why doesn't he have an Irish servant? Or if no one's willing to work for him, why not a slave? Heathens don't have priests badgering them about giving up slavery—they can have as many as they want with impunity. And they do, according to Father. They take slaves from all over the world. Father says you can hear a dozen languages spoken among the Norsemen's slaves. If this Norseman had an Irish slave, the lad could speak Gaelic to Irish customers. The Norse language is ugly.

Father speaks Norse, of course. He says Irish kings should these days. No town is safe from invasions by Vikings, and being able to talk with the enemy is essential. He says any man would rather get wealthy off you than kill you—so if you can bargain, good can happen.

I speak only Gaelic. That's enough for a woman, even a princess.

The silversmith wears a short purple tunic over trousers. Cúchulainn, the great hero of our Ulster tales, wore a purple mantle. Does this silversmith fancy himself to be as handsome as Cúchulainn? I'm almost embarrassed for him.

The silversmith looks at me inquiringly. He's very tall.

I walk past the belt buckles and sword hilts and pretend to be engrossed in browsing through the brooches on his display counter. His eyes heat my skin. I've never been close to a Norseman before. A common silversmith has no right to look at a princess like that. I lift my chin to confront his impudence with my own eyes.

He's polishing a large cup with two small handles, one directly across from the other. Enamel and glass stud it in the classic design of circles holding four petals in a star. It makes me think of my favorite chalice in our cathedral. It's lovely. This Norseman isn't the least bit crazy. He's no Viking.

And now I look at the pieces in the display counter more carefully. This jewelry is extraordinary. I would love to examine each piece carefully, slowly.

The silversmith picks up the brooch my eyes have settled on several times now. He pulls a length of black wool from a box and smoothes it flat. Then he places the brooch in the center. A darling four-footed animal—not a calf, nor a lamb, but something halfway between. Looping around the little creature are tendrils that curl into intricate leaves. The spirals caress the dear one. Almost like tongues.

A tingling sensation starts at my temples and runs down cheeks and neck, out shoulders, down arms, through ribs, around the curves of my flesh. I've never experienced anything like this before. It seems almost sinful. The sort of pleasure our abbot rails against.

I must have this brooch.

I fold my hands in front of my waist, as much to keep them from snatching the brooch as to appear ladylike. Are my cheeks flushed? Do my eyes shine? I press my lips together and swallow the saliva that has suddenly filled my mouth.

"I'm not allowed to bargain, sir," I say, hoping my tone of voice alone will carry the message, since I can't offer a single Norse word. "Please, set this one aside. I'll fetch my mother promptly. We have cattle. Sheep. Hogs. I'm sure we'll find an agreement."

"Certainly," he says in Gaelic, with a completely unassuming smile.

A fine salesman, indeed. The brooch is mine.

I step out into the street again, just as the shriek comes. High and sharp and bone-chilling.

"Brigid!" I shout. Oh, good Lord in heaven, is it her? "Brigid!" And I'm running up the road, and turning the corner.

CHAPTER TWO:
SUCCESSION

One scream. Then nothing. That's worse than a continual cry. I don't know where to look. I run frantically from hut to hut, thrusting my head through doorways, calling.

"Mel!"

I twirl around and Brigid runs into my arms.

"Oh, Brigid, I thought you—"

"I thought the same about you."

We hold each other in silence. She smells of horse. The livery. I should have known that's where she'd be. She loves animals. I hug her tighter.

Then fear breaks and we're swinging in a circle together, laughing, stupidly laughing in relief.

"It sounded bad," says Brigid. "Who was it, do you think?"

"Melkorka! Brigid!" Father's old manservant Aonghus comes hobbling up the street. "Come immediately." His face is stricken.

"What's happened?" I ask, as Brigid and I run to him, hand in hand.

"It's Nuada."

Nuada? That scream was Nuada's? My dear brother's? My heart thumps hard again. "What happened? Where is he?"

"We have to hurry."

Brigid and I race past Aonghus and onto the main street, where our chariot and the servants' wagon still wait outside the toolmaker's. Mother's maidservant, Sybil, stands with both hands over her mouth looking into the chariot through the window. Father has one foot raised, about to climb up beside Brogan on the driver's bench.

"Father!" Brigid reaches him first.

Father lifts her as though she's a tiny girl again. Brigid locks her legs around Father's waist. He looks past her at me, his mouth slack and open.

I run to the chariot and Sybil steps back so I can lean in the window. Nuada lies there, his head on Mother's lap, for all the world seeming dead. He's wrapped in Mother's cloak. It's soaked with blood.

"Nuada?" I say. "Nuada?"

"He can't answer, Melkorka." Fish eyes shine from Mother's pale face, round, unblinking.

"Is he . . . ?"

"Badly hurt. Yes. We must bring him to Liaig fast. You and Brigid will ride in the servants' wagon."

"What happened?"

"Go get in the wagon. Don't worry, Strahan will ride behind."

The cloak slips just a little. Nuada's arm shows. His right hand is gone. I step backward, shaking my head at this horror.

"Take her, Melkorka." Father passes Brigid to me.

I am stunned, unable to think, but his face contorts in misery, and I cannot refuse. He climbs up beside the driver and they're off, clattering fast up the wooden road.

I hug Brigid as hard as she hugs me.

"Is he dead?" she whispers in my ear.

I put her down just in time to lean over and vomit in the street.

Brigid cries. "Poor Nuada. Poor dead Nuada." She's got both hands in her hair and she's pulling. "Poor dead brother."

"He's alive," I say when I've got the air to speak again. "Thank the Lord, he is alive. But his hand got cut off."

"His hand?" Brigid wipes at her tears in confusion. "Which hand?"

"Does it matter?"

"His real hand?"

"That's all we have."

"It won't grow back," says Brigid. She takes a loud,

deep breath. And I don't know whether it's my smell she's just taken in or the news, but she leans over and vomits in the road too.

Sybil helps us into the back of the wagon. Then she climbs in herself. Aonghus is already there.

Torney sits on the driver's bench. He slaps the reins and our wagon follows the chariot. Strahan rides behind on his horse.

Brigid's crying again. She grabs at me. I make a tent for her of my arms and cloak, and lock her inside tight.

The wagon sways and bumps over rough ground, going faster than our stomachs can endure. Though they are empty, they continue to retch. I take off both our belts to try to make us more comfortable. It doesn't work. I push the straw on the wagon bed into plumpy seats for us. But the straw is wet from yesterday's rain. It's dense and hard.

Brigid crawls back into my arms again. I rock her, murmuring, "My little colleen, my little dear one, colleen, colleen."

She snuffles in a funny way and I realize she's fallen asleep. But I don't stop stroking her. I don't stop rocking. I don't stop murmuring.

✦ ✦ ✦

We drive straight through at a pummeling pace. Still, it's late night by the time we finally get home.

Sybil turns us over to the other women servants.

"Clothes off, young lady," says Lasair to Brigid.

Brigid sways on her feet, only half awakened. Her arms hang limp at her sides.

"Poor child. All right." And Lasair undresses Brigid.

Delaney does the same to me. I open my mouth to protest, but I close it again. It feels good to surrender to her hands. I was the big one in the wagon, comforting Brigid, comforting myself. But we're home now; I can be taken care of.

They wash us. Even our mouths are scrubbed out, though the action makes us retch again. Then clean, white night shifts slip over our heads and we're led to the kitchen.

Torney and Aonghus and Sybil and Brogan are already there. They look haggard from the journey. I must look haggard too.

I stiffen. It's not proper to sit at table with servants, and Brogan isn't even a servant, he's a slave—sitting with a slave is never done. But nothing is normal today. Brigid and I take our places and huddle together, as far from the others as possible.

We eat a soup of leeks and pigeon stock, milk, parsley,

and oats. Oats and barley are peasant grains, but Father likes them, so the cook makes them when we have no guests. Usually I prefer finer food, but I have no trouble eating now. The soup goes down heavy and burrows in my entrails, like a wounded animal.

As each person finishes, they leave, making soft shuffles through the rushes on the floor, until it's just Brogan and Brigid and me.

"Did you carry Nuada in, Brogan?" asks Brigid.

"Yes, little mistress."

"Did you see . . . ?" Brigid swallows loudly. "Did you see his arm?"

"Yes."

"Will it give you nightmares?"

"Brigid!" I say, shocked. "Don't ask such a thing."

"I'm past nightmares," says Brogan. "Before your father bought me, when I was still a boy, I was owned by a man who had a wicked temper. If a slave crossed his path when he was fuming, he'd cut off a part."

"A part?" asks Brigid. "What part?"

"An ear. A finger. Sometimes in his rage a hand or foot or—"

I clap my hands over Brigid's ears. "Enough, Brogan!"

"Sorry, mistress princess." Brogan leaves.

How dare he present such grisly images to Brigid.

How dare he compare a slave's mutilation to a prince's. But now my quick anger leaves as suddenly as it came. My hands fall to my lap. I shiver, though the night is not cold.

The manor house hushes. We sit a long while, silent.

Finally we go to the sickroom and hover outside the door.

Leather-shod feet slap softly as Delaney and Lasair pass in and out. Their basins are clean going in and brimming with bloody rags coming out.

The door is open, of course. A sickroom must have the door on each of the four walls open at all times so the ailing patient is visible from every direction. But we know we aren't allowed in until beckoned. And it's bad luck to look in before that.

We have hovered like this on other occasions. Usually we can hear well through the open sickroom door. But no one speaks in the usual way tonight. Whispers soak through the wood walls, reaching us only as a formless moment of heat.

"Come in, girls," calls Mother.

Of course she knew we were here. She knows these things.

We pad in. A bench has been pulled up beside Nuada's bed mat. Mother motions for us to sit there. We move quickly, in silent obedience.

HUSH

A servant passes by us and puts new reeds dipped in animal fat in the lamp, then hurries out again. Mother and Father stand on the other side of Nuada, with Liaig, our physician. They talk in hushed voices. Nuada's eyes are closed. A sheepskin covers him from the neck down. His face is pale in the lamp flicker.

Since Mother's eyes are on Liaig, I dare to get off the bench and lean over Nuada's face, hoping he'll let me into his thoughts. Nuada and I can tell each other everything just with our eyes and eyebrows—we've done it since we were small. We'd get punished for having plotted some trick together and be forbidden to talk to each other, so we learned to manage without words. But now his *máelchair*—the space between his eyebrows—lies flat; his brows are silent; his closed eyes, a secret.

His breath is sweet with mead. At least he's drunk himself beyond pain. His mouth moves, as though he's talking. There's a large mound under the covers by his right side.

Bent over like this, I can see Liaig's bag of instruments and medicines. It lies open on the floor beyond Nuada's head. A needle still glistens with blood. Long blond hairs coil beside it. Liaig has used strands of Mother's hair to stitch up Nuada. My lips go cold.

"It was a long ride," says Liaig quietly to Mother. "That

caused a great loss of blood." He taps the fingertips of one hand against the fingertips of the other in a nervous gesture. "The delay in treatment complicates the matter further." His tapping speeds up. "I cannot guarantee Nuada's fate."

My jaw clamps shut in anger. Nuada is Liaig's responsibility. Father had this sickroom set up exactly as Liaig told him it should be for the very best cure, regardless of the ailment. A rivulet of water runs across the middle of the floor. Slaves dug a trench and lined it with stones. They diverted the nearby stream into it. That way there's access to clean water at all times. Everything here is just right, perfect. Liaig has no excuse!

I drop back onto the bench and grab the edge on either side of my legs. I feel I'll fall forward if I don't hold on tight. I'm trembling now.

Brigid reaches out and lifts the edge of the sheepskin. I know I should stop her. Mother should be the one to reveal the injury. But I understand Brigid's need.

Nuada's right arm ends with a thick bandage where his hand should be. The bandage rests on a cushion.

Mother comes around the end of the bed and sits on the bench beside Brigid. She straightens the sheepskin over Nuada again. "It's gone. Nuada will show you for himself when he's ready."

"But how did his hand get cut off, Mother?" Brigid spreads her fingers wide and stares at her own hands as she talks. She clasps them together in a sudden, fierce energy and presses them against her chin. "How?" Tears stream down her face.

Though my cheeks are dry, I taste tears too. Deep inside me.

"I was in the back room of the toolmaker's, looking at the special collection." Mother's voice is level and tired. It seems she'll fall asleep before the next breath. Instead she pulls Brigid onto her lap and slides along the bench toward me. One arm around Brigid, one arm around me. "When he screamed, I ran to the front room. No one else was there. Nuada had passed out on the floor."

"But didn't he tell you everything later?" asks Brigid.

"He never got the chance. When he came to, he screamed with such pain, we poured mead down his throat and kept pouring."

"Will he be all right, Mother?"

Mother rests her cheek on top of Brigid's head. She doesn't speak. She seems defeated.

"Of course he'll be all right," I say in a defiant burst. I rub Brigid's hands within mine. "Why, old man O'Flaherty of Connacht lives fine, mean as a boar. And he lost his whole arm when he was just a boy."

"Which is why he never became king," says Mother.

The hair at the nape of my neck bristles. "What do you mean?"

"A true king must be perfect, *dianim*—without blemish."

I shake my head. My little brother has been bred to a certain future. He must have that future. "Nuada will be a perfect king. People feel calm when they hear him."

Mother's eyes widen. "You listen, Melkorka. Listen to yourself. Think about what you're saying. Maybe this is a blessing in disguise."

"I don't understand, Mother."

"Nuada couldn't have protected Downpatrick. He doesn't excite fear." She reaches out and touches Nuada's shoulder gently. "He couldn't be king. My sweet son."

"Don't talk like that!" Brigid's face crumples. "Don't say terrible things in front of Nuada."

"He cannot hear us, Brigid. He is senseless. But we are not. Despite our grief, we must be as sensible as we can right now." She sits tall and sets her jaw. "We must face the needs of our world."

"You're talking about the cursèd Vikings, aren't you?" My words come like a revelation. "You've always told us how horrible they are. We have to keep armies because of them!"

"The Vikings are wicked, yes," says Mother. "But if not

21

the Vikings, then another Irish king. Melkorka, my dear one, don't you know? Irish kings all die violent deaths, at one another's hands if not at invaders' hands. We're a bunch of squabbling families, stealing from one another."

"But then who will be King of Downpatrick after Father?" I ask.

"I don't know. We'll have to get together and decide. I'll let it be known that we're forming a council. Otherwise the monastery will try to impose someone on us."

"I know what," says Brigid. "Mel can be queen. She's older than Nuada anyway. We won't need a king."

A queen without a king? Me?

"Silly one." Mother sighs. "I'm queen because I married your father. The only way Melkorka will ever be a queen is if she marries an heir to a throne."

"But—"

"Hush now," says Mother. "Go to bed, girls. There's time enough to figure out the question of succession. Besides, your father is going to be king for many years yet."

I take Brigid by the hand and lead her to our bed mats, on the floor in Father and Mother's room. We pass an open window. The moon is bloodred. I rub my eyes, but the color stays.

Maybe the moon was just so two nights ago as well. I didn't look then. Maybe if I had, I would have seen the warning. I wouldn't have asked to go to Dublin.

I tuck Brigid in and crawl under my own covers. Maybe, maybe, maybe. My head hurts with all these maybes.

What actually happened? Was it an unfortunate accident? But it takes a lot of force to sever a hand. A tremendous amount. Was there an ax? Did a Viking wield it? I hate those heathens. All Norsemen are crazy. They're all Vikings, really. I hate them. I hate them.

Brigid tugs on my covers. I lift the edge and she crawls in beside me. I usually can't stand it when she joins me, she tosses so. But tonight I gather her in close. Her face is wet against my neck.

She's asleep almost instantly.

I can't sleep, though.

In the old days women fought alongside the men. Savage warriors, they say. But not these days, not in the year of our Lord 900. Women are exempt from military duty now, so hardly any of us fight. And even if we do fight, it's a crime to kill a woman in battle. The new laws treat us as though we're fragile.

But I'm not. I want to be in battle. I want to fight. I want to be killed fighting to protect my family.

Maybe I was the one who should have been born a boy, born to rule. Maybe little Brigid wasn't so silly, after all. Maybe, maybe, maybe.

CHAPTER THREE: WOMEN'S WORK

Feet scurry outside the bedchamber, quiet, quiet. So quiet my eyes pop open in dread.

I work my arm out from under Brigid and look around. Mother and Father are not on their bed mats. Nor are our personal servants.

I change into my tunic.

Should I wake my sister? Loyalty tells me she'll want to know everything I know. But it's barely dawn, and we had so little sleep, and she's only eight. And if it's the worst news, she doesn't need to hear it. Not yet.

I go straight to the sickroom and listen from outside. I hear Liaig.

"The fever struck during the night. If it gets much higher, he'll convulse. I've been waging war against it without stop. Without stop."

Father curses. He and Mother come out of the sickroom. They see me here, but they don't address me.

"If Nuada dies, we must avenge him," says Father.

If Nuada dies. Oh, Lord, where have you gone? My

24

eyes blur. *Digal*—vengeance—is the only way to restore honor. But it could do much harm. I've heard Father's reputation, though the last battle he fought took place before my birth: Father is a fierce avenger—*diglaid*. We could be at war soon.

"You do your part." Mother sets her jaw firm. "I'll do mine."

"I'll take Caley and Strahan. They're my best men. We'll find out what really happened." Father gathers Mother's hands in his and turns them palm up. He kisses them and buries his face there a moment, then he's gone, with loud footfalls this time.

I move close to Mother. "If we go to war, will it be with Vikings?"

"That depends on what your father finds out."

"But Dublin is a Viking city. It had to be Vikings."

"Dublin has decent Norsemen, too. And Irish. Vikings aren't the only vicious ones in this world."

My arms and chest go hot. "If there's a battle, I want to fight for Nuada. I want to be a warrior."

"Enough talk about women warriors." Mother walks toward the kitchen. "I have to alert the abbot."

I call out, "Women used to be warriors. . . ."

She stops. "Hush, I said. You need to learn when to hush, Melkorka. No talk now. We have a job."

"We? You and me?"

"And Brigid. Go wake her."

"What's our job?"

"Saving Nuada's life."

◆ ◆ ◆

Soon Brigid, Mother, and I set out on the mission. It takes us across the fort grounds, for our manor house nestles within the fort walls.

The fort is a depot for military supplies and a resting base for the town patrol. During time of attack, it can also serve as barracks for the fighters, like Irish forts everywhere. But, while typically no royalty lives inside fort walls, Father is a more cautious king than most, so he had our manor house built right here.

In the center of this stony walled area is a field. When I was small, we used it for agriculture. But now it's where cattle graze, with dovecotes at one corner.

We have more than three hundred pairs of pigeons in our two dovecotes. I rarely venture near the smelly things, but Brigid goes right in often, and collects eggs for custard pudding. The birds don't peck her, like they do the servants. They don't even scream at her; they let her take the eggs, just like that.

They're noisy this morning. And the smell is putrid. We walk by so close, I pinch my nose shut.

Men race past us, and older boys. Any male strong enough is assembling at the fort, waiting to find out if Father is going to wage war. News travels so quickly, it seems like magic.

The church is the first town building outside the fort walls. But Mother keeps walking.

"Why aren't we stopping?" asks Brigid.

"The abbot's conducting a special Mass to pray for Nuada's return to health. He's using the cathedral."

"So far outside town?"

"That way everyone can come—all the country folk as well."

The three of us follow the stone path to the livery and climb into a chariot and ride out the southwest town gate, over the double ditches. Windmills on the grassy hills spin like children cartwheeling.

We pass clusters of *clochan*, homes the poor live in, set on islands the people have built of earth and stone in the marshes. They aren't wood, like those of the well-off families in town or in the defended farmsteads ruled by vassals or lesser kings—the ringforts. They're stone-and-mud ovals, dug half into the ground. The roofs are thatched. I look at them and think of beehives, of the people inside crowded together in the dark—only one door, and hardly any air.

On the far side of the river, stone walls separate fields from one another. In the summer I love to come out this way. Breezes sway the oats, barley, rye. And corn, yes, corn is the best to see then, tall in the sun.

Thank you, Lord. Thank you for making this stretch of Eire the most arable land of the entire country. The taxes the farmers pay to our town on all that harvest keep my family rich.

Right now, though, it's barely the start of spring. The fields are used for grazing. The field walls stand tall enough to prevent sheep from leaping over them and dense enough to prevent rats from getting through.

Our chariot stops for slave boys driving a sheep flock from their night enclosures across to those fields, where they'll tend them all day. The boys have perhaps a month left of this routine before they'll urge the flocks along the droving lanes farther into the countryside to graze on wild grasses by day. Then other slaves, male and female, will plow with oxen and sow the fields. They'll tend them and harvest them, swinging those big sickles.

I think of the abbot standing in the entranceway of the cathedral and looking out on these fields. He preaches that slavery should be banned—and, of course, he means Father should ban it. He tells us, again and again, the story of Saint Patrick, our patron, who was born on the other side of the Irish Sea five hundred years ago and snatched from his home, stolen as a slave. For six years Saint Patrick herded pigs—just like those boys are herding sheep—before he escaped.

Father answers without hesitation. He says trying to rid the country of slaves is as pointless as trying to rid it of fairies. They are part of the fabric of Irish life. After all, no one would be rich without the work of the slaves. Including the church.

And then there's silence on the matter for the next few months. Until the abbot preaches again.

I can't decide what I think. But now Nuada is on my mind—and so I remember what happened last year. Nuada was offered a *cumal*—a female slave—for three cows. He didn't buy her, but he came home and told me. His eyes glittered with anger. He said civilized people don't own other people.

I couldn't believe he turned down such a good offer. But now I hope Saint Patrick remembers that Nuada didn't buy the slave girl. We need him on our side today.

Our chariot stops a second time for three more slave boys and many more sheep. I've never known a smart slave. Some are of ordinary intelligence, but most are stupid. Saint Patrick was a smart slave, though. Other-wise he would have died a slave.

And maybe Brogan is smart. I think of what he told us last night about his previous owner, that brute. It wasn't proper that he spoke so crassly in front of Brigid and me. But the very fact that he got away impresses me. Where was Brogan stolen from originally? I know he was a child when it happened. He told me once he was part of a group of children and women whisked from a hillock. That's how he said it—whisked. I didn't ask him anything then. Does he miss his mother? Does he remember life before he was a slave?

I watch for signs of intelligence in these boys cross-ing the road, but not a one returns my gaze.

The chariot at last pulls up in front of the cathedral and we enter. The nave is already crowded with veiled heads, women's heads. The men are few and elderly, naturally—given the assembly at the fort. We walk to the front, before the altar.

The air stinks like sheep. No one is wearing a cloak this morning, the weather has warmed so. Instead they have on long-sleeved tunics. And the tunics of the peas-ants are wool, not flax, of a quality nowhere near as refined as what my family uses. From the stench, I wonder if the wool was even washed properly before it was spun.

The displays of saints' relics that line both sides of the cathedral are practically empty. The bishop took most relics on a circuit about a month ago, to raise consciousness among the rural people. And to raise money as well, of course. Donations of every sort. Silver.

I hate silver now. I wish I'd never wanted a silver brooch. I wish I'd stayed by Nuada's side. I wish his hand was safely on the end of his arm.

I bow my head, but I can't listen. Mother was wrong: It's not our abbot performing the ceremony. It's the bishop. He says he hurried on horseback from the far northern edge of Ulster to be here just for this Mass. He says how fortunate he was to have heard of the royal disaster in time to get here. He goes on and on about the glory of my father's reign, whining like an insect drone, distant and increasingly incomprehensible. I know he's doing his best. I know he's trying to help Nuada. But I cannot force my attention to his words. Besides, now he's turned to Latin. Nothing makes sense.

And nothing matters but the heat inside my brother. I stand, kneel, stand, swallowing my screams. Please, sweet Lord, please don't make my silly desire to see Dublin cost my family so dearly. Please spare Nuada's life.

After the Mass, we take off our shoes and set them in the chariot. We walk, with the chariot following. Most of the women who were at the Mass accompany us, walking behind, barefoot as well.

We pass the cemetery, and Brigid points. "There are the burial stones you love to sit on. With that ugly script."

"Don't say that. All writing is holy, because Christianity brought writing to Eire."

"You're quoting Father again. I hate it when you do that."

"All right, say what you want about the Roman alphabet. But those stones have ogham script. Don't speak ill of ogham, Brigid. Please. It's used only for sacred texts, whether Gaelic or Latin. So it must be the Lord's way of writing."

It even looks sacred, with all those little lines coming off long ones, like feathers. I feel like a bird when I perch on those stones. I wish I could perch there now. I wish I was free of guilt, free enough to fly away.

We walk as the sun burns the fog off the hilltops.

"It's so far," says a girl.

"The pebbles hurt," says another.

"Are we there yet?"

The younger girls go on and on.

I look at Brigid. My sister walks with purpose. Not a complaint passes through her determined lips. I move close and we lock hands.

We arrive at the rocky summit of the hill where Saint Patrick is buried and fall to our knees and pray out loud. The bishop hasn't come. This is only women's voices, calling to our patron saint, appealing from our special, intimate relationship with him to intervene on Nuada's behalf.

Please, Saint Patrick. I make so many mistakes that I have no right to ask for favors. But Nuada has always been so good. Oh, please, prevail on our Lord to save my dear brother.

We get into the chariot again and head back past fields of ferns, burdock, and purple thistles, toward the shore. I'm surprised. I thought we would go inland to Armagh. That's the headquarters of Irish Christianity, after all.

I'm about to ask where we're going when the question becomes irrelevant: The tall belfry of the monastery at Dunkeld looms ahead, with its huge, rectangular-cut stones. Oh, yes, of course, Mother is right. It would be presumptuous to go to Armagh. Going to Dunkeld shows our humility. Lord, see how humble we are, please. See how sorrow humbles us beyond anything else.

The monastery has so many dwellings built around it that it's really a settlement. Almost a town. We are greeted and led into a small dining room, where we eat a thin stew with monks who don't talk to us. Their shaven heads make them look like slaves.

Mother finishes her bowl and leans toward one of the elder monks and whispers. She stands. "Go on, girls. Go walk, so we can talk in private."

Brigid and I leave, but slowly, intent on catching the beginnings of the conversation.

"Succession," says Mother, "is a royal matter, not an ecclesiastical one."

I blink. Mother always gets right to the point. But I thought the point would be asking them to pray for Nuada. Instead she has come as queen of Downpatrick, to establish her rights in the choice of a successor for Father.

For an instant I'm off balance. Mother moved so quickly from the role of God's humble supplicant to the role of haughty queen. I remember her words last night: We must be sensible now. I admire her ability to steer straight.

I pull Brigid by the arm and we wander from table to table in the scribe room. A manuscript is clearly in progress on one of them. The pages have not yet been sewn together.

"Irish illuminated texts are prized all over the world," I say. "There are only two good things the Norsemen have done for us. They taught us how to make better fishing boats. And Vikings have taken stolen Irish goods and sold them everywhere, as far to the east as Persia—"

"I know, I know, I know." Brigid pushes a stool up in front of a table holding a particularly large manuscript, open to the middle. "The world comes to us to trade now. They know we have superb workmanship. Particularly in the monasteries." She climbs up onto the stool. "Stop quoting Father and tell me a story."

I stand beside her and look at the text. This script is in Latin, I know, so even if I could read, I wouldn't be able to understand the words. But the pages themselves are stunning just to look at with those illustrations. I can give it a try. "All right," I say, "pick a page."

The open page has pictures of mice eating the communion host. I hope she doesn't pick it. I have no idea what I could say about it.

Brigid carefully turns two pages. "This one."

The illustration is of a man with a halo. Peacocks flank him, and there are chalices with vines twining around them at all four corners. The colors are marvelous: green from copper, yellow from orpiment, red from some Mediterranean insect. The Gospels in the great book at the monastery in Armagh are boring compared to this. They are nothing but brown iron ink.

The man in this illustration carries a sheaf of papers. The Gospel, I'm sure. So this could be Matthew, Mark, Luke, or John. But there's no lion with wings and no eagle—so it's not Mark. Ah, his feet are bare. "I think that's Saint Luke."

"Well?" Brigid looks at me. "Come on. Naming him isn't a story. I want a story."

Saint Luke is the patron saint of physicians. We want him on our side today too, not just Saint Patrick. If I tell his story well enough, maybe he'll intercede for Nuada. "Once, in Greece, a baby was born. I think it was Greece, at least. It might have been—"

"You're not supposed to say 'I think' and stuff like that. Just say 'Greece' and get on with it. Tell it big."

"He was a slave. The family who owned him educated him in medicine so that he could be the resident physician for the family." I stop.

"Well?" says Brigid. "And then?"

"And then he became an apostle. And he wrote the Gospel. And he told stories none of the other Gospel writers told." I stop again.

Brigid makes a face. "I hope he told them better than you do."

"He loved poor people. And women."

"All men love women."

"Like you know anything about it," I say.

"I heard Brogan. That's exactly what he said."

"Brogan is a slave."

"So what?"

"Slaves are ignorant, Brigid."

"You just said Saint Luke was a slave, and he became a physician."

"He was an exception."

"Well, then, what about Saint Patrick? Everyone knows he was a slave."

"Don't be absurd. He was a saint. All saints are exceptions."

"You call everyone I name an exception. That's cheating, Mel. Slaves seem like anyone else to me. Some are ignorant and some aren't."

"You make me tired, Brigid."

"I'm more tired than you. I want Nuada back. You couldn't tell a good story to save your life."

"We're not trying to save my life today. Did you forget?"

Brigid's eyes tear up. "Oh."

"I'm sorry I said that. Listen, Nuada will be well soon, and he'll tell us lots of stories."

"You promise?"

I push my hair back from my temples. Last night I

sat in the sickroom and declared Nuada would be all right. But that was before the fever took him. Now I'm unsure of everything.

"It's all right," Brigid says softly. "I hate false promises more than I hate bad storytelling."

We leave the library and pass a three-sided shed that exudes the stench of excrement. One monk presses filth on a calfskin. I know about this: the excrement loosens the hair. Another monk stands by a frame with a calf-skin stretched on it and scrapes the last bits of hair off it with a knife that comes to a wide end rather than a point. They're making vellum for the pages of their manuscripts. How beautiful works can start from such revolting slime is part of the mystery. Or that's what Father says.

We go out and sit beside a large stone cross with carvings, also in Latin. We wait and wait. The sun weakens.

Finally Mother appears. She takes us each by the hand and we get into the chariot and go home. We don't talk on the way. Soon Brigid is asleep with her head in my lap. I envy the way she can use sleep to escape. I have no refuge. Nor does Mother. She wrings her hands continually.

As we cross the bridge through Nun's gate on the

north side of town, a servant comes running. I hold myself rigid against the news.

"The fever broke."

Mother cries. I collapse against her side.

Women's work has prevailed.

CHAPTER FOUR:
COMPENSATION

Nuada is going to live. He's awake now, though hardly lucid, since he's plied with spirit drinks every moment. Nothing else can dull such severe pain. And he still cannot tell us what happened. He says he doesn't know. An ax came down on his hand. He saw the blade. He saw his hand severed. That's all he remembers.

Still, he is lucid enough to enjoy a party, a celebration that he will live. That's what we're preparing.

"On such short notice," says Mother, "we'll have to settle for a wandering bard." Which, her face says, means a man of lesser skills. This is a disappointment, for poetry is the highlight of a party.

"If you please, my queen, not so," says Strahan. "There happens to be a famous *filid*, a poet of the noble class, visiting in Armagh."

"Indeed? Well, summon him immediately."

"Stories," says Brigid. "Not just poems, Mother. We need lots of stories. *Seanchais*—storytellers. Nuada loves stories much more than poems."

"Of course."

Brigid is jumpy all the rest of the day. I admit I am too. I may be bad at telling stories, but I love listening. From *Samhain* to *Beltain*—November 1 to May 1—we welcome itinerant storytellers, who give much pleasure in return for a meal and a pallet to sleep on. They help us pass the rainy nights of winter and early spring. Oh, this will be a fine party if only the slaves can work faster. Mother and I have to nip at their heels, there are so many blankets to rinse and pots to fill. Usually banquets take days of preparation. But all we have is one.

The guests begin arriving by midmorning of the next day. By midday, a cow and a pig have been slaughtered and roasted. The aroma makes even the air tasty. Beer and wine and mead flow freely, each guest taking according to his taste.

And, now, finally, the evening entertainment begins. Horns, pipes, whistles, harps—every corner of the main hall rings with music.

The *filid* marches in and stamps the floor importantly with his wooden staff. The bells on it jingle loudly. Then he plays a sharp tune on his *feadog*—his metal whistle.

Mother stands beside Brigid and me. "In the old days," she whispers to us, "these poets were druids, who knew secret ways for contacting other worlds."

41

"What other worlds?" asks Brigid.

"Spirit worlds. The poets told the future and cast spells. Even today they can make themselves appear mysterious if their audience wants them to."

"I want him to," says Brigid.

Mother gives a look of mock surprise. "Really?"

The *filid* begins, plucking on his lute. His eyebrows rise, his cheeks puff, his nose wrinkles, all to emphasize his points. But alas, his first poem amounts to nothing more than genealogies. He uses the same sounds over and over, praising the history of various chiefs and kings of Ulster.

I had hoped for verse about visions and elopements and true love, especially true love gone athwart. Or, if not that, then at least cattle raids and battles and heroism. Genealogies make me fall asleep.

But our guests cheer raucously when they hear their ancestors honored. I watch Liaig cheer too, though he looks about to fall over. He's exhausted, after caring for Nuada without stop.

Father and Mother and Brigid and I leave our contented guests with the *filid* before the first poem even draws to an end. We troop eagerly into the sickroom.

Nuada is quite tipsy, it's obvious. He sits on the bed mat propped up on cushions. His right arm is raised.

Liaig says that will help slow any residual bleeding, and cut the pain, too.

But it can't be cutting the pain much. Nuada's index finger of his left hand is curled through the handle of a jug of beer, just as it was yesterday. He takes swigs frequently. Sometimes the muscles of his jaw twitch. His eyes are glassy, his cheeks flushed.

I look at my hands and wince. If one was gone . . .

"Are you sure you want *seanchais?*" asks Mother.

"Absolutely," says Nuada. He spills beer on his chest. I'm not convinced he even knows what he's answering. His eyes haven't talked to mine since Dublin.

I take my place on the bench beside Nuada's bed and sit on my hands. Brigid sits beside me. Mother and Father take another bench, nearer the fire.

"When . . . ?" says Brigid.

But a *seanchai* comes in before she can finish her question. There are several in the hall, as at any royal party, but the one who enters now is my favorite. He's as correct in tone and style as any noble *filid*.

He plays the hammer dulcimer as accompaniment, like a minstrel. He begins. "Cúchulainn had a special—"

"Stop," I say. "Please." My ears hurt at the name Cúchulainn. I think of his purple mantle and the purple tunic of the silversmith in Dublin, hateful Dublin. I can't bear it. Tonight is for celebrating. Nuada will live. Tonight is a happy time. "Please tell of someone else."

All eyes but Nuada's are on me, wanting an explanation.

"Someone who doesn't battle."

Mother looks at me with surprised approval. She makes a little click of her tongue, a sign of agreement.

The storyteller begins again. "Gartnán is a rich man. A chief of a *crannóg*. Picture him. Picture this chief of his settlement in the middle of an island in a lake. Shut your eyes and picture him.

"Do you see this *crannóg* serving as a homestead for a few dozen people? Do you see them toiling hard, scraping to get by? Do you see them cold and hungry in winter? Do you see them riddled with stinging insects in summer? Always scrabbling, always suffering?

"Ha! You pictured wrong. Gartnán's island is no ordinary island; it's huge, enormous, colossal. It's a world in the middle of a lake. The fields stretch so far, it takes seven plow teams to prepare them for sowing. The meadows are filled with seven herds. Each herd has seven score cows. Big beasts. Big contented lowing beasts that give enough milk to fill the lake seven times over.

"Gartnán has fifty nets for catching fish, and another fifty for deer. These are big fish, big deer. A family can feast on just one fish for seven days; the entire *crannóg* can feast on just one deer for seven days.

"The fishnets hang by ropes from the windows of the giant kitchen. Each rope ends in a bell on the rail, right in front of the steward. When the salmon run, the bells ring. They ring so loud that trees fall and the heavens shake. Four men stand in the river and throw the netted salmon up into the hands of the steward.

"And you're wondering how the steward can hold such fish? Use your brains. Your good Ulster brains. See him. See what a massive man he is?

"Oh, our Gartnán leads a charmed life, he does. He's no ordinary rich man. Wealth flows from his body like sweat from a slave's.

"He has the entire island gilded with red gold. And he lies on his couch, drinking mead.

"Mead, my friends, my good fellows. Mead." He laughs. "And that's exactly what we should do now." He lifts one of the mugs waiting on the table at the foot of Nuada's bed and drinks deeply. "Now, that was a Gartnán sip."

I have heard this story in various forms all my life, but it never fails to stir my innards. Such wealth in a simple *crannóg*. The Lord takes care of royalty on Earth.

We all drink mead and congratulate the storyteller.

And now he sets aside the dulcimer and rubs his

hands together as if warming them up for the next tale. He will stand by the hearth and paint pictures in our head till dawn, if Nuada can stay awake that long.

"Prepare yourselves for a tale of fairies and elves." His voice swirls around us like rushing waters, enchanting us instantly. "Can you hear them? Can you smell them? Can you sense them? Hiding in the corners. And behind the chests."

We look in the corners. We stare suspiciously at the chests.

He laughs. "But that will come later. For now . . . draw your mind back fifty years." With flat, open hands, he makes circles in the air over his right shoulder, going back, back, back in time. "A hundred years, three hundred years, to the year 600, to the dense forests, the primeval forests. Are you there? Listen. You hear birds, insects, the swish of animals through the leaves. Listen. Can you hear laughter? Can you hear the merriest laughter you've ever imagined?"

I hear it.

"That's Finn. Finn and his warriors rule this forest."

A messenger comes through the door right then. Father jumps to his feet and his face shows he's been expecting him. "At last!"

Mother stands too.

"King Myrkjartan." The messenger bows repeatedly while he catches his breath. "The Norseman Bjarni has the information you seek about the recent misfortune."

"I'm waiting," says Father.

"It was the act of a foolish boy."

"Nonsense," says Mother. She grabs Father by the arm, but her eyes are on the messenger. "How could a boy have the strength to do such damage?"

"Not a little boy," says the messenger. "A youth of fourteen."

"A Norse youth?" asks Father.

"Yes. He got into a dice game, lost whatever he had, but kept on playing." The messenger hesitates. "So the winner demanded he chop off the hand of a Christian slave as his payment."

"A slave?" yips Mother. "Nuada hardly looks like a lowly slave."

"Of course not. His clothing bespoke riches. But they watched him a moment from the doorway, and his meek demeanor—"

"Nuada's demeanor is kind, not meek!"

The messenger nods in agreement. "Boys in a dare make mistakes."

Outrageous words. To cut off Nuada's hand instead of a slave's!

"The winner is as much to blame as the youth, then," says Mother.

"Bjarni agrees," the messenger says quickly. "They'd been drinking too much."

"Tell us the details," says Mother. "Exactly what happened?"

Brigid takes my hand and squeezes. I sneak a glance at Nuada. He stares at the bedclothes. I can't tell if he's listening. I can't tell what he's thinking, what he's feeling.

"Your son was—"

"Prince Nuada," says Mother. "Have the courtesy to use his name."

"Prince Nuada," says the messenger, "was looking at a tool on a wooden bench. He leaned forward, his hands splayed to either side like this." The messenger demonstrates. "His right hand was in a perfect position. The youth simply came up behind and swung the ax. Just once."

I see it in my mind. Poor Nuada, standing there, then *slam*, the ax comes down from nowhere. Like a curse. The brutality makes everything go black for an instant.

"He grabbed the hand and ran," continues the messenger.

"And destroyed our son's future in one cruel act." Mother sinks back onto the bench.

"What is the youth's name?" says Father.

"Bjarni will not reveal that. Nor the name of the winner of the dice game—who was also just a youth."

"They won't get away with it," says Father. "This act will not go unpunished."

"Bjarni asks that you think not in terms of punishment, but, rather, compensation."

"Compensation?" says Mother. "Don't you people require blood for blood? How about having that boy's hand chopped off?"

I gasp at her words. But of course it's only fair.

The messenger blanches. "Bjarni is ready to compensate well for the indiscretions of the boys." He slips a satchel from his shoulder, gets down on one knee, and dumps the contents on the floor. Gems glitter.

Mother stands and stamps a foot. "This is outrageous. He offers us his loot."

"Wait," says Father. "Don't say things you'll regret."

"You can't hush me! Does this Bjarni think we're idiots? He's stolen these gems from Irish monasteries."

Father shakes his head and looks at the messenger as though he's asking for commiseration. "This is what it's like to be married to a headstrong woman."

"The Vikings are the most vengeful of all," says Mother. "If anyone understands revenge, they do. Why should a Viking expect us to withhold punishment?"

"For a very important reason," says the messenger. "Families shouldn't deal in punishment."

Mother shakes her head in confusion.

"Explain yourself," Father says sternly.

"The gems are only part of the deal." The messenger licks his lips nervously. "They are to ensure the wealth of Prince Nuada his whole life long. But Bjarni has another offer—and this one is to ensure the happiness of your family."

"Our son has been mutilated," says Mother. "And you talk of an offer that can bring happiness?"

"He asks for your daughter, Princess Melkorka, in marriage."

"What?" Mother's hand goes to her throat as though she's being strangled. She looks at me.

I am staring back at her. This cannot be happening. I am the one being strangled. I run to her and stand half behind her.

"Bjarni has wealth beyond your dreams," says the messenger.

"Does he live in Dublin?" asks Father.

"Don't ask!" screams Mother. "Don't you dare ask. Don't you dare consider that offer."

"And don't you say another word," says Father. I've never heard him use such a tone with Mother before.

"There are things I must know. You can listen. All of you can listen. But if you say another word, any of you, I'll make you leave the room."

Mother lowers herself slowly onto the bench. I sit beside her. Brigid comes and sits on Mother's lap. We cling to one another.

"Bjarni lives in Nidaros, at the mouth of the River Nidelva, way up the coast of Nóregr, the Norse land." The messenger raises his hand in the air as though he's painting the north country for our imaginations. "He's here visiting."

"Raiding," says Mother under her breath.

If Father hears, he doesn't show it.

I press my knees together till it hurts. Everyone knows the stories about Viking towns up in the north country. Nidaros and Bjørgvin and others whose names I forget, but that are just as horrible. Wealth means nothing there. The whole lot of them might as well be disgusting peasants, for, rich or poor, they are all filthy heathens with unspeakable rituals. A slave in Eire has a better fate than a queen up there. The thought of living with such brutes—no, no, it's unbearable.

"Are the boys who harmed Nuada in Bjarni's family?" asks Father. He talks in a normal voice. As though this whole conversation is not horrific.

"Not in his family," says the messenger in a barely audible voice, "no."

"But from his town?" asks Father.

"Yes."

"And where are they now?" asks Father.

"In Dublin, visiting, like I said. They came for the winter. But they're leaving next week. For the southern parts of the Nóregr."

"All of them?" asks Father. "Bjarni and the two youths?"

"Yes. And Bjarni wants to take Princess Melkorka with him." The messenger looks at me. "She's assured a life of luxury."

"How did he choose Melkorka?" asks Father.

"He saw her on the streets of Dublin. All in red. The day of the accident."

"It was no accident," Mother hisses.

"I have a counterproposal," says Father.

The messenger nods. "I will bring it to Bjarni willingly."

"Tell him the act of these two youths has changed the destiny of our family. Nuada is my only son."

Mother puts an arm around me. I sit tall to hear more.

"Tell him that a room full of gems wouldn't be enough to compensate. Making my daughter his wife is a better attempt at compensation, but an irrelevant one. Melkorka is beautiful, and she would soon be married to an Irish king anyway."

Good for Father. He's standing up for us. He has always hated Vikings. We will go to war against them, rather than accept their shameful offer.

"Tell him, however, that I am a reasonable man. I loathe violence. If he truly wants to compensate, he must assure us that Melkorka will live the life of a queen. That's what she'd have here. It's her due. And he must throw a party on his ship the night he comes for her. An extravagant party. I'll send fifteen women of my kingdom to keep his men happy. I will pick them myself."

Mother forms a fist and bites her own knuckles. Brigid is crying. But I do nothing. I have turned to stone.

"And tell him to have three more satchels of gems brought to me. Immediately."

CHAPTER FIVE:
FEAR

Father closes the door behind the messenger. Then he closes the three other sickroom doors. That's against Liaig's rules. We are just the family now.

He turns to us. "Get a good night's sleep."

"*Mairg ar maccu*—woe to our children." Mother's voice is flat. "Have you gone mad?"

"My brain has never functioned better."

"You're selling me," I cry, finally finding my voice. I sit hunched in a ball.

Mother puts her hand on my back. "You want your daughter to bed down with an animal? You want our grandchildren to be *Gall-Gaels*—half foreigner, half Irish? And then you promise fifteen girls to frolic with those savages. We are Christians; have you forgotten? Oh, King, your brain isn't functioning at all."

"I'll run away." I sit up straight as I speak, fighting off dizziness.

Father gives a little laugh. "You? Where would you go? The contemplative life of a convent would never do for my daughters. And you couldn't serve anyone, taking orders."

"Don't scold her. Don't you dare." Mother's words come strong. "You've turned against us all. You're the one acting inexplicably."

"Not a single girl of my kingdom will get on a Viking ship," says Father.

Have my ears heard right? I push my hair back and listen hard.

"Tomorrow you will gather a group of women. No slaves. No servants. Only your closest friends. You'll make tunics that will fit fifteen men and dye them colors, like women wear. And you'll stuff them in the right places, to make the right curves. Next week fifteen Irish soldiers will meet Bjarni's Viking ship." Father paces, rubbing his hands together. "Our soldiers, dressed as maidens— why, you can even add some of Brigid's ribbons to their long hair—they will go on board and greet the Norsemen with smiles and hugs. And slay the entire lot of them."

"The two youths will be on that ship," says Mother with slow realization. "The youths who harmed Nuada."

"Exactly," says Father.

"A heinous plan," says Mother. "And one they deserve. We will avenge our son." She looks over at Nuada.

Nuada's eyes are unblinking.

"It must be kept secret," says Father. "Only the women who sew the dresses, only the men who wear them—only they can know. The word must not get back to Bjarni, or he will launch a preemptive attack."

"Of course," says Mother.

"Do you understand, girls?" Father squats before Brigid. "When Vikings attack, they come in huge numbers. They steal, burn, kill. This is a secret unlike any other of your life, Brigid. You must not speak of it to anyone."

"I won't, Father." Brigid puts her hand on his head. She's done that since she was small. "But after the Irish soldiers kill the Vikings, won't other Vikings come to avenge them, too?"

"They'll never know what happened. We'll kill all the men on board and sink the ship. When others come to ask, we'll say the ship never arrived." Father stands now. "I'll act indignant that my daughter and the fifteen lasses were left in the lurch." He puffs out his chest. "If they act suspicious, I'll accuse them of disputing my word and demand they pay the fee for abusing my honor. Vikings know how we Irish feel about our honor. That will be the end of it." He turns to me. "You'll be safe, Melkorka."

I stare at him. The word "safe" makes no sense. "Your plan puts everyone at risk."

"Their offer put us at risk. And you two girls will be far from here. Your mother will dress you as boys and send you away." Father opens the four doors of the sickroom. "Like I said before, get a good night's sleep. You'll need it."

Brigid and I crawl under the bedcovers together again. And, again, she falls into slumber easily.

Mother and Father enter quietly. So do our personal servants. And everyone sleeps. Except me. My mind plays tricks in the dark.

What if there's a traitor among us? A dirty supporter of the Norsemen? I pull at my hair.

What if Father's soldiers are recognized as men right off? The Vikings will have time to grab their weapons. Swords, spears, shields, arrows, knives. And, of course, axes. I saw Viking weapons in the toolmaker's in Dublin. I may have looked upon the very ax that severed Nuada's hand. The angry Vikings will kill the soldiers, then march into Downpatrick and kill everyone else. Except the women. The women's fate will be worse than death.

We have to make the men look just right. I'll give them lessons myself on how to walk like girls. The "maidens" can carry jugs of mead and pour them down the Vikings' throats. Everyone talks about how Vikings get so drunk they stagger and fall off their ships and perish in the sea.

What if someone escapes? A single Viking who makes it back to the other ships could be our ruin.

And, oh, where will Brigid and I go while all this happens?

I toss hard. Finally I get up and walk outside. The chill of deep night makes me small within my cloak. Winter has returned for a final lashing before spring.

I climb the outside stairs to the top of the east fort wall. The steps are irregular in height, so that attacking strangers cannot run up them without stumbling. But I know them by heart; I climb without falter.

Up here the winds whip my hair across my mouth. The sea is turbulent tonight, white wave-tips shining in the moonlight. I think of the famous poem:

Is acher in gáith innocht
fo-fuasna fairggae findholt.
Ni ágor réimm mora minn
dond láechraid lainn ua Lothlind.

(The wind tonight blows harsh
and spews the white sea foam.
My heart need not fear Vikings
crossing the Irish Sea.)

I haven't grown up fearing Vikings. Hating them, yes, but not fearing them. Not like my parents.

Mother tells how the seas were infested with Viking pirates when she was small. She talks with revulsion about how many Viking settlements there are now in Eire. Not just Dublin, but Wexford, Cork, Limerick, Waterford.

Father, likewise, goes on and on about Viking raids. They get their gold and silver, their precious stones and chandeliers, from monasteries, where our kings stored them for safekeeping. They loot, then burn the Lord's buildings. They've even put entire ecclesiastical communities to the sword.

It was hard for my parents to agree to my birthday request. Oh, wretched Vikings, who ruined everything.

When Mother and Father were small, they scanned the sea for invaders, quaking. This poem that they recite with fervor never meant much to me before. But now the rough sea signals safety to me. No Vikings will attack tonight.

But I'm not safe. None of us are. I hug myself and keep my eyes wide, though the drying wind burns them.

The sea is black, but in the day it is so many shades of green. And the hills have even more variations on that hue. Grandmother used to say there were forty shades of green in Eire, from the tears of invasions.

I hug myself tighter.

"Who goes there?"

I turn to face a soldier. He holds a spear at the ready. It's surprising that the patrol didn't find me sooner. Discouraging. This is a moment when our guard has to be at its most competent. My stomach churns. I lift my hands in surrender.

"Princess Melkorka? Is that you?"

This man is only a head taller than me. And his hair is almost as long and has even more curls. Were it not for his forked beard, he could be taken for a maid. Yes, I think he could.

Will he be one of the fifteen? I feel instant pity for him. Father should send slaves instead of fine soldiers.

"Melkorka, Princess?"

"Yes."

"What are you doing here?"

"Entertaining nightmares."

The soldier opens his mouth, then closes it. "Shall I accompany you home?"

"Please."

CHAPTER SIX:
HORSEBACK

We're in the main hall, one week after Nuada's hand was severed, preparing for our revenge. Fifteen soldiers dress in tunics. They already have ribbons in their hair—Brigid tied them, carefully making bows. They practice walking like women in a line behind me, but they exaggerate too much. They look like fools. Lord, protect these fools. Let no one die. No Irish man.

It's afternoon. The men wait their turn to be shaven clean. Father wanted it done late, so that their cheeks will be as soft as possible when they hug the Vikings later today. They munch on wheat bread. It's a luxury, a food for kings at festivals. But Father said all fifteen of them deserve to be treated like kings.

Nuada walks through the soldiers, holding his stump high in the air to prevent bleeding. "Take care of one another," he says to a group, but listlessly. He should be more excited; everyone is risking their lives for our honor, after all. But I know where to lay the blame. In this past week he has been recovering well, but he's still drunk most of the time. It's the only way to combat the pain.

Mother enters and beckons me over. "Find Brigid and meet me in the kitchen."

It's easy enough to find Brigid. I saw her swipe a handful of ribbons and run off with them not long ago. And I know for a fact that the biggest sow had piglets yesterday.

I take the stone path to the small farmyard within the fort walls. The hens cluck like crazy things as I come up.

The old dog staggers over to greet me. I scratch him behind the ears. "Where're the piggies, old boy?"

He follows dumbly at my heels, as I head to the muddy area the pigs prefer.

And there's Brigid.

The sow struggles to her feet at the sight of me, her fat rolling. Sucking piggies dangle from her and fall away with pitiful squeals. She has such a nasty disposition, that one. If she would act a little nicer, she'd be in the house now, like other nursing sows. Only that sow can't be nice. Not to most people.

But she was just lying there for Brigid, still as a dead thing. How my sister does it, I don't know. Animals simply trust her, even the most unpleasant ones. They know she loves them.

Two piggies have ribbons tied around their ears. Brigid smiles. "Want to help? There are six left to do."

The sow takes a threatening step toward me. The piggies squeal louder.

"Come. We have to meet Mother in the kitchen. Now."

"All right." Brigid kisses the closest piggy and we run together back toward the manor house.

"You smell like that farmyard," I say.

"What a surprise." Brigid laughs.

She knows tonight's the night. But if she's thinking about it, she's better at acting than I am. Maybe she has Father's gift of deception. I can barely keep my hands from flying all around. I can barely keep my tongue from shrieking.

We pass the milking yard and the sweet-sour scent lures me. I want to go in there and stand between brindled cows. They're nothing like pigs. They bump against each other, completely docile. After an initial glance at you, they hardly seem to know you're there. It's like you disappear.

A blessèd thought.

"It's time," whispers Mother, as we come through the kitchen door. "Time to hide."

"Where are we to go?" I ask.

"I already told you."

"All you said was a safe place. You keep putting me off. What safe place?"

"It's not far. I'll give you directions when you're on the horse."

"I want to know now."

"Hush, Melkorka. You really do need to learn when to hush." Mother looks around warily and I realize she's afraid we might be overheard. "Here." She holds up tattered, somewhat dirty tunics made of coarse nettle. Peasant clothes. "Change. And hurry about it."

"They're shabby." I draw back, wrinkling my nose. "And they smell. I wouldn't be caught dead in such things."

"Exactly." Mother shakes the larger tunic in front of my face. "Even if people look you straight in the eyes, they won't recognize princesses in this garb."

My cheeks flame. Of course. But those rags repulse me.

Brigid grabs the smaller tunic in a flash. "It will be like a game, Mel. Come on."

I want to slap her for being the first to obey, for acting so cheerful. I have to bite my tongue not to say something nasty as we change clothes.

Mother pulls us by the hand out through the fort gate and behind a thick bush. A fat mare waits there. She's not one of ours.

Mother undoes the ribbons from Brigid's hair, then ruffles up both our heads, so we look messy. She kicks at the dirt till the wet underneath shows. "Here." She smears the cakey mud across Brigid's nose. "That's enough for you. But Melkorka, you need a lot. You've become a beauty. And right now, beauty is your enemy. Go on."

Mother called me a beauty. And when Father was talking to that messenger the other day, he called me beautiful. I warm inside. But how can I? I shouldn't be lingering on such words in this moment, not now.

I hurry to take a handful of mud and draw it down one temple and across my cheek and chin. I won't be sluggish anymore. I'll be quicker than Brigid. I'm the older one, after all.

Mother nods approvingly. "Like that, on this nag, no one will ever guess who you are." She makes a cup of her linked hands. "Put a foot in here and climb up."

"I haven't been on horseback in years, Mother."

"It's easy," says Brigid.

"That's why you'll ride in front," says Mother. "You'll control the beast, Brigid. And there won't be much controlling to do. This mare's gentle. But she can go fast if you need her to."

"My tunic will ride up," I say. "My legs will show."

"Which is fine for a boy. You'll be safer as boys—two peasant boys. No one will bother you." Mother cups her hands insistently before me.

I take the lift, and up, I'm on the horse. It seems high. I swallow and look down and swallow again.

In a flash, Brigid's in front of me. "Give me the reins, Mother."

Mother unties the reins from the hitching pole and hands them to Brigid. Then she slops a blob of mud on my exposed knee and runs it down to my ankle. She hesitates at my shoe.

"Please let us keep our shoes, Mother." I won't go barefoot like a slave. "Please."

"Go out the south gate and take the fork that leads to the coast."

I circle my arms around Brigid's waist. "But that's the direction of Dublin."

"Exactly. If Vikings come looking tonight, they'll expect you to have fled inland. To the monastery. Or north. Any direction but toward Dublin."

"Where should we stop?" asks Brigid.

"The convent," I say quickly, gratified to know something Brigid doesn't. Once Mother said south, it was obvious. "That's right, Mother, no?"

"A convent will protect you from Irish criminals, but not Vikings. Vikings see a convent as an opportunity. No, stay on the coastal path till you get south of Carlingford Lough. Then turn inland. Soon you'll come to a ringfort.

It's large. The chief and his wife, Michael and Brenda, they'll take you in."

"So they know we're coming?" I ask.

"No. No one knows. I couldn't take the risk of a messenger."

"What if we don't make it that far?" I ask.

"You will."

"What if we don't?"

"You will."

"What if Michael and Brenda have left or been overthrown? What then?"

"You'll use your good sense, Melkorka. You'll present yourselves as lost boys and beg for charity."

"What if they aren't charitable sorts?"

Mother gives a mirthless smile. She hands me a small cloth pouch on a string. "Hang it around your neck inside your clothes. Your gold teething ring from when you were a baby is in there, Melkorka. Any nobleman will realize it's worth several years' lodging and food for both of you. And anyone who isn't a fool will recognize it as belonging to the first child of a truly wealthy king. It's worth generations of loyalty. You'll be taken in."

Mother holds another pouch up to me now, this one large. "There's plenty to eat as you travel to that welcoming ringfort. Stay there till you hear it's safe to come home."

And what if we don't hear that? What if we hear that Downpatrick has been burned to the ground? But I won't ask that with Brigid listening. She's only eight.

If the worst happens, I'll think of the right thing to do. Because I'll have to. Brigid depends on me.

"And Melkorka, don't show your teething ring till you know you can trust someone. And don't reveal who you are to anyone."

"Not even Michael and Brenda?"

"No one." She grabs my arm. "*Immalle*—together—whatever you do, stay together." All along she's acted solid, in control. But now her lips give her away. They tremble.

The skin on my arms pimples like gooseflesh. We might never see Mother again. "I love you."

"I love you too," chirps Brigid.

"*Immalle*," says Mother.

"*Immalle*. I promise, Mother."

"Go fast. God speed you with my love."

Brigid turns the mare with mastery that doesn't surprise me. But then she pulls the horse to a stop. "Where will you be?" she calls back to Mother.

"Right here. Don't you worry. Vikings don't want anything to do with an old woman like me." She waves. "Go now. As fast as you can."

"You're not old," says Brigid.

It's true. But I hope Brigid is saying it just to please Mother. I hope she doesn't realize Mother is in danger.

"Let's go," I say in her ear.

We ride out the town gate, take the left fork, trot along the coast.

✦   ✦   ✦

It's a sunny afternoon. It has no right being so clear and lovely when anything could happen, anything terrible. The ground is dry and easy underfoot. The mare goes quickly. This part of Ulster is hardly populated. Once we pass the convent, there won't be any settlements before Carlingford Lough. So we have to make it there. Did Mother judge the distance right?

But she must have, for it seems like hardly any time at all has passed when we're already circling the east side of the Mourne Mountains. The lough is just beyond them. Downpatrick has mountains around it, with good pastures in the middle. Father says it's like a miniature version of all Eire, which is ringed by mountains, with a bowl-shaped plain in the center. I like that idea. That means the people of our kingdom are as Irish as Irish get.

"I'm hungry," says Brigid.

I don't want to stop yet. There isn't that much day-light left. "Don't you think we should go a while more?"

"No." Her voice is like a rod striking metal. I can hear the worry.

Night will make everything so much more difficult. But we can't be that far from the lough now. And Brigid is eight. "You're right," I say reasonably. "We'll be able to ride faster once our stomachs are full. Let's find a place among the trees to picnic."

We slide off the horse before I realize that I don't know how we'll climb back up again. My heart skips a beat. But I'll figure it out. Like Mother said. Later.

I look through the trees and choose an oak to tie the mare to. In the food pouch is cloth filled with *millsén,* a cooked cheese made of sweet sheep curds. It's flavored with honey.

Brigid purses her lips and points. "What's this?"

A large hunk of rye bread is folded in another swath of cloth.

I see my chance to redeem myself for all the com-plaining I did to Mother. "Don't be a brat. It's better than most peasants get. I like the taste." I take a giant bite.

Brigid grabs the bread from me and tears into it. She chews big. "We're peasant boys."

"For a while at least."

She grins.

That's when we hear it, both of us at the same moment.

Brigid's grin disappears.

I rush to the mare and pull her body radial to the tree trunk and behind it, so that no one in the ship that's passing can see her. I lace my fingers like Mother did and give Brigid a boost onto the mare's back.

"If they see us," I say, "if it looks like they're stopping, I'll hand you the reins and you ride inland as fast as you can to the first ringfort you come to."

"I won't go without you. Mother said *immalle*—together."

"Don't be stupid, Brigid. I don't know how to get back up."

"Don't you be stupid, Mel. Climb the bloody tree."

There's a branch at just about the right level. "And I thought big sisters take care of little ones," I say with false lightness.

"Sisters take care of each other."

We peek out from behind the tree, Brigid on the horse and me in front of them, and watch the Viking ship pass in the placid waters. They're singing. They'll be at Downpatrick before dark, the rate they're going. But they're singing. Maybe the very thought of the women

HUSH

ahead made them start the festivities early. Maybe they're already drunk. Oh, Lord, let them be drunk.

I feel something light on my head, and I realize it's Brigid's palm. I put my own hand up on top of hers, and I swallow.

The ship passes without noticing us. Thank the Lord for the good forests of Eire.

Brigid slips to the ground again and I divide up the sweet-curd cheese.

Brigid puts her left hand on the dirt and lets a beetle crawl over it, while she chews lazily.

The bread smells so pleasant, and Brigid looks so peaceful, I want to stay a while. But dusk is upon us.

"We should hurry if we want to get there before nightfall."

I untie the horse and give Brigid a boost up. Then I hand her the reins.

I climb the tree, careful not to break branches. Between Brigid's good maneuvering of the mare and the cooperation of the branches, I manage to wind up behind her.

Dusk brings a chill. I wrap my arms tighter around Brigid's waist.

The forest recedes a little from the coast. We trot through brambles and ferns and burdock and thistles.

They give way now to evergreens that sigh in the light wind. The tangy smell prickles my nose. The earth is hard-packed here, not soft, like in Downpatrick. The path is windswept. We can go a little faster. We travel in silence, each sealed inside our heads.

But it isn't silent really. The noise of the horse's hooves covers any noise we might have heard from the sea. So when the boat appears beside us, I'm so shocked, I clamp my teeth down and bite my tongue.

A man on the deck waves to us. He waves and waves as they pass.

"What should we do?" asks Brigid in horror.

"Nothing. It's too late to hide."

The boat came from behind; it travels from the north. So it was already almost past when we saw it.

This is a different kind of boat, though. Like the first ship, it's long and narrow, with oar holes down both sides. But there are two masts for the square sails. And there's a half deck with a cabin on it. Plus there's no dragon head on the prow.

"It's all right," I say. "They're not Vikings. Look how different the boat is. It's all right."

"But we didn't see them," says Brigid. "They saw us first, Mel."

"I know."

Brigid's middle expands within my arms. She's breathing extra deep. "We're not good at this."

"We'll get better," I say. "I'll look back over my shoulder. You look forward. We won't be taken by surprise next time."

"I don't want a next time." Her voice rises in a whine.

"Calm down, Brigid."

"No. I want to stop."

"What do you mean? Where?"

"Anywhere. I don't want to stay on this path."

She's right. The path is too visible from the sea. It's far more dangerous than I had realized. The alternatives are dangerous too, though.

"If we leave the path, we risk getting lost. We might not find Carlingford Lough. We might not find the ringfort Mother told us to go to."

"I don't want to go the ringfort," says Brigid. "I want us to stop now and sleep in the forest. You and me, together. *Immalle.* And go back home in the morning."

We can't go back till it's safe, I am thinking. But better not to say that. "We don't have blankets, Brigid. Night is still cold."

"We have each other." Her voice screeches almost out of control.

"Listen to me. It's easy to get lost. We have to stay near the coast. Do you agree?"

"I want to stop."

"Listen to me. Do you agree?"

"Yes."

"All right, then. I agree with you, too. Together we can figure anything out."

"*Immalle*," says Brigid.

"Yes, *immalle*. We'll leave the path."

"And we'll stop."

Once we leave the path, we'll be so slowed down, we'll never get all the way to Carlingford Lough tonight anyway. "All right."

CHAPTER SEVEN:
STONES

"*Du-mem-se*—protect me." It's a whisper, from Brigid. Is she awake or talking in her sleep? And to whom? But I'm the only one to hear. I sit up and lean over her to listen closely. Her breath is regular; she's asleep.

I climb out of the corn kiln. It's full night. The sudden chill sends a shiver down my spine. I realize this kiln has been offering us a fair shelter. No wind comes through at all. I had no idea the temperature had dropped this much in the little while that we've been inside.

Every corn farmer has a kiln, of course. Eire's rain would cause mold and ruin a corn harvest if the farmers didn't dry it in a kiln before milling. So kilns dot the countryside. But this kiln was abandoned long ago, from the looks of it. And whatever farmstead it served is likewise gone. We're lucky, I suppose, that it's still tight, though I can't wait till this is all over so I can get back home to comfortable sleeping quarters instead of dirty old kilns.

I give the mare a pat. She's awake, grazing in the black

of night. Brigid insisted we weight down her reins with a large rock, so that she'd have almost the full length of the reins to graze. If we'd tied her to a tree, she couldn't eat as much as she wanted. Especially since the nearest trees are pine with essentially no undergrowth.

I walk to the sea. It's not more than two hundred paces. I look up the coast. All I see is land and water meeting stars.

What is happening in Downpatrick now? If there's fire, I can't see it from here, no matter how hot it burns, no matter how much smoke it makes; we're too far.

Dear Lord in heaven, keep my family safe.

◆ ◆ ◆

When I wake again, I climb out of the dim kiln and lean my forehead against the stone side. I'm weary still, for my sleep was shallow and disturbed.

What happened in Downpatrick last night? Did Father's plan work? How many died? And who?

The stone digs into my skin. I step away and turn around to look at the world about us.

Early morning dances in a haze over the small lake in front of me. I didn't even realize there was a lake here last night.

A speckled fish jumps. A lark sings. A wind comes up from the south, soft, with welcome warmth. I feel charmed.

The urge to run grabs me. I want to go fast. But a few steps teach me the nasty fact: I'm sore from yesterday's ride. Really sore.

I look around for the mare and notice the big rock that held down her reins is turned on its side. Prickles of panic sting my temples.

A cuckoo calls. I swirl around and see on the other side of the lake a peat bog that comes practically clear to the shore. And there's the mare. Standing at least a foot deep in the bog. The stupid thing wandered in and can't get out.

I've walked in a bog before—I know that awful feeling. You fear you'll sink forever. Gone, with a mouth full of mud. The mare's probably as panicked as I was just a moment ago. She doesn't dare take a step.

The walk around the end of the lake should be quick, but the way I have to walk, legs spread, makes it longer. The mare holds her eyes on me as I approach. I click with the side of my tongue. Men in liveries do that, so it must work.

It doesn't.

I call to her. I sing. I shout.

I pick up a stone and throw it as hard as I can. It lands beside her with a soft plop. I throw another and another and another. The dumb thing is still too scared to move.

"Hold on, will you?" whispers Brigid, appearing at my side like a fairy child materializing out of the air. She's rubbing sleep from her eyes. "Go on back to the kiln. I'll get her."

I walk backward, watching what she does.

She does nothing. She stands and looks at the mare. Then she takes a step along the lake shore. One step. She waits, never taking her eyes off the mare.

And the mare actually takes a step.

Brigid takes another step. She waits.

The mare takes another step.

They continue like that till the mare finally slogs out of the bog onto the shore. Brigid picks up the muddy reins and leads her into the shallows. She washes off the mare's legs. Then she brings her around to me.

"How do you do that?" I ask.

Brigid shrugs.

"Really. I want to know. How do you get animals to trust you?"

"You don't do it by throwing things at them." She smiles.

I laugh in spite of myself. "I didn't start out throwing. I clicked to her. And called. And sang."

"There's your error. A horse doesn't click or call or sing. Animals don't talk. So you don't talk to animals. You keep your mouth shut and watch them."

"Silence with the animals," I say.

Brigid hands me the reins. "Is there any food left?"

"No."

"You were right," says Brigid. "You said last night we should save some of it. I'm sorry."

"It's all right. We can't be far from that ringfort now."

"No." Brigid shakes her head in that stubborn way I know too well. "I don't want to go to a settlement. I want to go home." Her voice gets sharp. Her eyes are already liquid. It always takes me by surprise, the way she can be so grown-up one second and such a baby the next.

I don't know what makes me look at the sky right then, but I do. I grab Brigid's arm and spin her to face south.

Her mouth drops open, her eyes widen in wonder. "How many do you guess there are?"

The storks stretch back as far as I can see. Father says that in spring and summer there are more white storks in Eire than there are people. They spend the winter in hot Africa. But they come home to breed and roost. I love to see them. They say storks are the best parents; they'll be consumed in a fire rather than abandon a nest. If it's true, it's a piercing truth.

"How many?" asks Brigid. "Hundreds?" She bounces her finger on the air as she points at them in an attempt to count.

This one mustering is thick and wide, covering the wetlands like a feather blanket, so many it's dizzying. "Thousands," I breathe.

They land with loud flapping, hopping from trees to the ground, then walking around us on pink-orange legs with their straight, red-orange bills pointed down. Many of them tower over us. We're enveloped.

Every now and then those long necks straighten with a snap as their bills poke the mud. I think of snakes striking, and I pull Brigid to me. I've never seen a snake, of course. There aren't any in Eire. But I've seen their images in the Gospel book at the Kells monastery in Meath. Father says snakes can kill with one bite.

"They're eating." Brigid's tone is authoritative. She's back to being grown-up, not the least upset by being in the middle of a mustering. "Frogs."

"Ew." I shudder.

She gives a satisfied laugh at my reaction. "They eat rats and lizards and just about anything. But they love frogs best. That's why stork feet are always wet."

I hug myself and stand very still. A loud rattle comes from a stork to my right. Then another near him. Then from all directions. They're throwing their heads back and clattering their bills. Swan bevies can make you practically deaf with their trumpeting and hooting. But I realize now I've never heard a stork make a peep, just this bill clatter. I practically shout in Brigid's ear, "And why are they silent?"

"Silent?" shouts back Brigid with a grin.

"You know, why don't they use their voices?"

"It's something to do with their throats." Brigid cocks her head at me, and her eyes twinkle teasingly. "Did you think the vampire Dearg-due had struck them mute?"

I slap her shoulder, but not hard. I'm only half-annoyed.

The rattling stops as suddenly as it started.

"We'd better get going," I say as gently as I can. "We have to get to the ringfort and stay till word comes that it's safe to return home."

"Home," says Brigid. "I want to go home. I want to know what happened."

"I do too," I whisper. "But Mother said."

Brigid's face pinches with disappointment. "Storks bring good luck." She walks very slowly toward the center of the mustering.

Well, all right, we can spend a little longer here.

I walk out of the mustering, and now I notice nests in the trees. Last night I thought the trees were particularly thick, but it was just all those nests. This mustering must return here every spring. I imagine them cleaning out the old nests and patching up holes. And I get an idea.

I go to the closest tree with a nest, climb level with the top edge, and shimmy out a branch till I can look down into the nest. A human family could fit inside, it's so deep. But a human's weight would crash through.

I don't have to climb in, though; what I'm looking for is easy to snatch.

Three big feathers are caught in the far edge of the nest. With black on them—wing feathers.

I hold on to a nearby branch and lean farther. My fingertips graze one, but I can't grasp it.

I look down. It's not that far. I might not get hurt even if I do fall. I clasp a branch with my left hand and lunge across the nest, trying to stay clear of the swarming lice, and I close my right fist around feathers as I realize I'm falling. Dry sticks jab me. I thump on the ground and roll.

When I finally stop shaking, I smile. The three feathers came with me. And all it cost was scrapes.

I hold them up to the sunlight. What looked all black

from a distance is highlighted with a sheen of purple and green iridescence. A proper present these are. Something to delight Brigid with the next time she's on the verge of crying. I tuck them inside my tunic.

"Brigid, my colleen," I call.

She comes running—she's finally ready to leave too.

"We'll find that kind family—that Michael and Brenda and whatever children they have—and we'll eat something good. What would you like? What would be lovely?"

"Dried apples," says Brigid, putting on a brave face.

I smile.

She smiles back tentatively. "Dripping with honey." Her eyes search mine.

I smile harder for encouragement.

She grins now. "Not liquid or chunk honey—but creamed honey. The best."

"Bread dipped in hot sheep milk," I sing.

"Cakes fried in pig fat!" crows Brigid.

I can't top that. "We could try to catch a salmon if we had something to use as a net."

"Or crayfish. I love crayfish."

It's a happy dream. But we have no nets.

We mount the mare, through the help of an ash tree this time.

"Whoa," I cry out. "Aren't you sore, Brigid? Please go slow."

Brigid laughs. But she pulls the mare to a walk.

It's slow going without a path. But I know we're heading south because the sun is to our left—and this is the direction the birds came from. And I'm pretty sure we're staying close to the coast. Whenever the trees permit it, I look through for a glimpse of water.

Very soon we emerge from the trees on a large lake. Carlingford Lough, for sure. The ringfort Mother told us to go to is a short ride up the other side of the lake.

Within moments we spot a stone mound. We stop and watch, cautious. I know what it is—a hermit's dwelling. It's made without any mud at all, just well-fitted stones. There's no sign that it's used, though. The grass around it isn't matted anywhere. We walk the mare as quietly as we can.

"It's abandoned," whispers Brigid. "There could be food."

"Not a chance," I say. "And it's bound to be nasty inside. Besides, we'll be at the ringfort soon."

"I'm hungry now, Mel. Please, let's look."

I'm hungry too. And Mother misjudged how long it would take us to get to Carlingford Lough. Maybe she misjudged how long it will take us to get to the ringfort from here too.

"All right. There won't be anything edible. But there could be a fishing net. Listen, Brigid. You stay on the mare's back. I'll get down and toss in a stone. If anyone comes out, you race off and I'll run after you."

"You can't run. You can hardly walk. I saw you. You're sore from riding. So I'll be the one." She slips off the horse before I can stop her. She grabs a stone and throws it through the low entrance.

I hold my breath.

But nothing happens.

Brigid throws a handful of stones. Then she stoops over to peek inside. "It's dark. Come help me."

I slide off the mare and tie her up, to a tree this time—I won't make the same mistake twice.

We can stand easily inside, but it's dark. A capstone covers the smoke hole, and that makes it so dark it feels safer to go on all fours. We touch our way. It's dry and cold and messy with old animal scat. We're standing now. But the walls are no better than the floor. No food, of course. But no net, either. No tools. Not one useful thing.

Brigid crawls out first.

I give a last wistful swipe of my hand. Nothing. But that's all right. We're almost at the ringfort.

I duck out the door behind Brigid, straight into the hands of a large, hairy man.

My scream is cut off by the cloth he ties over my mouth. I kick as another comes over my eyes. In seconds my hands are roped together behind my back. I buck and kick out behind, but someone takes my elbow and jerks me along.

Where is Brigid?

I smell clay. The man who pulls me is pungent with it.

Nearby I hear feet tramping, struggling.

Brigid?

Where is Brigid?

PART TWO

CHAPTER EIGHT:
PRISONERS

I'm pulled into water. Up to my knees. Now my thighs. Waves lap at my belly. Deeper.

I yank against the hand on my elbow. The man's fingers dig into me. They cut. Long fingernails. Claws.

Deeper.

I won't be able to swim with my hands tied behind my back.

I kick at him, but the water slows me and my tunic gets caught in my legs. I fall and swallow salt water and choke on this gag in my mouth.

His grip on my elbow never loosens. I'm pulled up and dragged along, slogging, slogging through sea.

I will die in a peasant's tunic. If anyone finds my body, they won't even know who I am. If Mother and Father live still, they will never know what became of me.

I see nothing inside this blindfold; I strangle inside this gag.

Deeper.

I yank, and kick, and fall, completely underwater this time.

I'm grabbed around the waist from behind and lifted out into the air. The smell of clay on this man overwhelms me. A voice from above shouts in a foreign language.

The man who holds me, the one who stinks of clay, shouts back.

I'm thrashing like a caught fish.

Hands grab at me from above and I'm dropped onto wood. I feel the planks on my arms as I roll.

More shouts. Another wet thump on wood. Brigid? The floor moves under me.

This is a ship.

I crawl as quickly as I can toward the thump I just heard and I slam into someone. The person lets out a garbled cry.

With no hands or eyes to help, I cannot even tell if this is man or woman. But it's not Brigid.

The boat lurches. I knock into someone else. And another. Muffled yelps. And it dawns on me: These people are gagged like me. Probably blindfolded as well, with trussed hands. Maybe people from my own Downpatrick.

I stop and lie still. Beyond the noise of wind and fluttering sails, I hear them bashing into things, falling, struggling to get up. Now and then someone tries to speak. The distorted cries rend my heart.

Someone shuffles by and I hear the smack of flesh on flesh, a cry of pain, a loud thud, gulping groans of agony. Someone trips over my feet and lands beside me, weeping. A woman's noises.

My bottom suddenly warms with hot liquid. I stand quickly. My nose tells me the woman urinated. My tunic was already wet from the sea, but now it's filthy.

And I need to urinate too.

A man shouts in my face. His breath is sour beer. The words aren't Gaelic, and it doesn't seem like the little Norse I've heard. Who on Earth is he? I thrust my face forward and would shout back if only this gag weren't here.

A punch to my ribs. I crumple to my knees. My forehead slams on the deck.

I give in to darkness.

+ + +

The wind is cold. I don't know how long I was unconscious, but every part of me aches from having been in an awkward position for so long. It must have been the whole rest of the daylight, for the air feels like night.

With much struggle and pain, I work myself up to sitting. My rib cage hurts. Every slight pull of my tunic over that stretch of chest makes me flinch. I fear a rib is cracked. This crew gives wicked blows. Who are they? What right do they have to abuse us like this? My jaw clenches in anger.

Many people in Father's kingdom have never traveled. But I have. And all the long journeys except that one damnable trip to Dublin have been by boat. Even journeys inland, since much of our countryside is impassible except by river. I know what happens on a ship. I am blindfolded and gagged, but there's still much I can figure out.

I strain to distinguish sounds. Fluttering comes from two separate sources. So this ship has two sails. Two. Viking ships have one. This isn't Bjarni's ship, then. The other prisoners might not be from Downpatrick, after all.

Maybe Mother and Father and Nuada are all still alive, and Downpatrick is safe. Oh, Lord, let that be so.

Two sails. The second ship that passed us last night had two sails. A man on deck waved to us. That ship was going south.

The motion of the waves combined with the wind tells me land is to our right—starboard; so we're heading south.

If it's the same ship that passed us, it must have

stopped for the night right after seeing us. Almost as though it stopped just in order to lie in wait for us.

But that makes no sense. What kind of ship would have stopped to wait for Brigid and me?

Someone pulls at the knot on the back of my blindfold. He yanks my hair in the process. I twist to slam my head at him, but the searing pain in my rib stops me cold.

I blink and stare down at nothing, then up at the starry sky. It's the middle of the night.

The man who took off my blindfold is now untying the blindfold of a woman beside me. She must be the one who urinated. The one who wept. He's rough with her, too. He's short, with a dull, mean face. The woman looks at him and cries again. She gets to her feet.

He leers at her and brushes a hand across her breasts.

Lord.

I haven't cried. And now I'll make sure I don't. For all intents and purposes I am a boy.

When my eyes adjust to the dark, I make out bodies farther away. Some are still blindfolded.

Brigid! She's but ten paces away. A mixture of sadness and gladness washes over me. I wish she had escaped. But at least we're together. *Immalle.*

I get to my feet. Lord, how it hurts to move.

The leering man unties Brigid's blindfold. She blinks and our eyes meet. But she quickly glances past me.

I slowly, carefully, sink back to my haunches. My broken rib stabs at my innards. I sit and count the others, breathing shallowly to cut the pain.

It's hard to be sure, because so much obstructs my vision, but by my best reckoning there are eight prisoners. Two adults—women, I think. The rest of us, children. The crew outnumber us, but not by much. They're moving about, adjusting the sails, fiddling with gear, so they're even harder to count accurately.

Three of the children clustered together as soon as their blindfolds came off. They're trying to talk to one another. The gags make it impossible, of course. But they don't stop. Stupid peasants.

The last child's blindfold is now untied. The child runs and falls. He buries his face in the tunic of the other woman—not the weeping one.

My eyes grow watery. I blink and turn my gaze to the water. A choppy, unforgiving sea separates us from the far-off shore. And, oh! It's on the port side. What?

I stand again—Lord, what pain—and look starboard. No land there. As far as I can see, nothing. Are we really going north again, back toward Downpatrick?

But now I see white cliffs! My heart thumps so

loud, I can't hear anything else. What a fool I am. We're nowhere near Downpatrick. We've been sailing fast. It must be past midnight. The sky is turning rosy off to starboard. It's close to dawn.

And the timing is right; if we went south and then crossed the Irish Sea and circled around Wales and headed back up the channel, it's possible that those could really be the famous white cliffs I've heard tales of.

This ship is on the southeast side of Saxon Britain. Never in my life did I expect to be this far from home. The enormity of the distance undoes me. What on Earth is going on? Where are we going?

We have to escape. We must get off this boat right now, before it gets any farther from Eire.

If our hands weren't tied, Brigid and I could jump overboard and swim for it. We're both strong swimmers. We swim in the river near the monastery. And we swim in Strangford Lough in summer.

But the sea's so cold.

And that shore is far.

And my rib is cracked.

And our hands are tied.

I feel heavy and stupid and absent. As though I'm nothing but a pile of dirty clothing, no better than the other poor slobs on this boat.

CHAPTER NINE:
MORE PRISONERS

Morning mist makes me shiver. My tunic is still damp from being pulled through the water. Brigid's must be too. I assume a wide stance so the wind will dry me.

A crew member walks to the center of the deck and bangs on a metal box. He shouts at us in that ugly, unknown language. He's short too, but much wider than the leering one who took off our blindfolds. All our eyes are uncovered now, all are on him.

He pushes down on the crying woman's shoulder till she sits. We understand; those of us standing now sit.

The wide man pulls a basket out from under an animal-hide blanket. It's a hickory basket, the kind you find all over Ulster. He reaches in and grabs a handful of light-colored things. He drops one on each prisoner's lap. They're parsnips. Boiled parsnips. Peasant food. And these are filthy. I can see dirt still pressed in their skin—disgusting. My empty stomach clenches against my will. I salivate on my gag.

The wide man goes from prisoner to prisoner, taking off our gags now. People groan in relief.

"Mother," cries one of the children in a huddle of three, as the gag falls away. "Mother, help me."

Neither of the two women responds. And the child doesn't look at them, anyway. He doesn't look at anyone.

The man removes Brigid's gag now. Her eyes flicker toward mine, then away immediately. She turns her back in silence, without even a groan. I must call to her. As soon as this cursèd gag is off, I'll comfort her.

The wide man removes the gag from the peasant woman across from me. She twists her head and bites him on the shoulder.

He shouts and clubs her across the face with the back of his fist.

Her mouth bleeds. "Dirty devil!" She spits blood on the man's arm. "God will punish you for this!"

The man grabs the parsnip from her lap and throws it on the lap of the next prisoner, a child. This is the child who ran to that woman as soon as his blindfold was removed. That peasant woman must be crazy. Her hands are tied. What did she think she could do besides enrage the man? Now she has no parsnip.

The child's eyes look wild. He bows his head quickly

as the crew member ungags him. He doesn't move. He doesn't make a peep.

Finally I am ungagged. I glance at Brigid. She's staring at me. The instant our eyes meet, she looks down. There's fierceness in her face. She's trying to tell me something. I wait to see if her eyes will speak again, but she doesn't lift her head. Why won't she look at me? For all the world, it's as though she doesn't know me.

But, of course! Brigid is clever. If we're lucky, the crew won't remember that we were taken together. So long as we do nothing to remind them, they won't be expecting us to act like sisters. And that could give us a slight advantage. I turn my face to the sky and my heart bangs in excitement; it's good to have a smart sister.

And her silence is smart too. She didn't make a groan when her gag fell away. Probably she's holding her tongue because these men are animals. The man who took us, the stinking man, is worse than an animal. He's a *beithíoch*—a beast. Brigid won't talk around him. That's her rule with animals. But silence is also a part of our deception, because our language would give us away as being from the same place.

I won't speak either.

A crew member comes around holding a beer jug. It's

the leering one again. He puts it up to the lips of the child near me. My own thirst now scrapes my throat raw. It's absurd to be this thirsty in just one day. But I am Melkorka. I am a princess. I will not beg with any gesture of face or body. I try to sit tall, but even that small movement causes me to flinch. The skin over my ribs has swollen; I sense the puffiness.

At last the jug comes to my lips. I drink as deeply as I can before the leering man takes it away. Blessèd beer; it slakes the thirst, and, once it gets deep within, it will dull the pain in my chest.

When the leering man comes to the crazy woman, he hesitates and says something in that infernal language.

"I'll bite you, too." She bares her teeth. "Devils, all of you! You'll all roast in hell."

The other crew member, the wide one that the crazy woman bit, the one who uses his fist as a club, says something to the leering man with the beer jug, who moves on to the next prisoner.

That woman is insane. No parsnip, no beer. You'd think she was a deranged princess, the way she's so haughty. Except for her peasant talk.

Now the wide man—who I think of as Club Fist— unties our hands. All of us except the crazy woman.

I have neither blindfold nor gag now. And my hands

are free. Brigid's are too. I look toward the land. I can only gaze upward, because the side of the ship comes higher than my level line of vision. But I can still see that, though the white cliffs are past, the coast remains steep and very far. Even if we made it there, where would we climb ashore?

I eat my parsnip. It's salty.

The child beside the crazy woman looks around. His eyes take in my face but don't linger. He's already eaten one parsnip. He holds the other in his hand. Now he jerks that hand quickly toward the crazy woman.

She takes a big bite of parsnip.

The child's hand is back in his lap in a flash. It happened fast.

I wait to see if a crew member will punish the boy. A child that size couldn't take a blow like the one I received.

But nothing happens.

The boy's eyes are scanning everyone again. I cannot believe this; he saw Club Fist hit the woman. He knows what can happen.

His arm jerks out again. And again the crazy woman takes a big bite. That child is as crazy as the woman.

Another crew member, one with a long mustache, shouts at the boy and comes lumbering over.

The mustache man grabs the rest of the parsnip and eats it himself.

And that's the end of it. Crazy woman, crazy child. My breath comes back.

A man calls out. I look. It's the man who captured me, the one who stinks of clay. The crew gather at the rear, near the tiller. They eat. I can't see the food, but I smell it. Cold roasted goat. I salivate again.

When they finish, Clay Man says something to the group of three children and points to the waste pot. One of the boys obediently uses it. Then the other children do. Even Brigid. She acts just like the others—a perfect little peasant. The small boy who fed the crazy woman lifts her tunic for her as she sits on the pot, because her hands are still tied.

And now it's my turn. My cheeks flame, but I follow Brigid's example, meeting no one's eyes. Deception is far more important than this disgrace. And such a minor thing cannot truly sully the soul of a princess. At least our tunics rest on our thighs and offer a vestige of privacy.

As each of us get off the pot, the mustache man ties our hands again. And now the leering man and Club Fist gag us. But they leave us without blindfolds.

Clay Man shouts to the crew. He's definitely in charge.

The crew members go to their stations. Some work the sails. But some row now too. Sails and oars together. Clay Man must be in a sudden hurry. Why?

I look around. But the sea is empty; the shore is empty. He's not rushing from anyone.

So he must be rushing toward something.

The oars clunk in the oar holes. *Clunk. Clunk.* Something deep inside my head throbs in the same rhythm. I am nothing but a beat. *Clunk. Clunk.*

I sink to the deck, wincing with each movement, and curl up small.

✦ ✦ ✦

Clattering wakes me. Two boys come tumbling headfirst into the boat. They knock things aside, fighting and flailing in their hysteria. Their hands are tied behind them. They are gagged and blindfolded. They wear only crude Saxon britches and those britches are soaked.

They must be thinking they've wound up in hell. And they can be at most only twelve or thirteen. Younger than me, I'm sure of it. What were they doing outside without shirts on? Senseless fools.

One of them knocks into the crazy woman. I expect her to push back violently. But she only tilts her head sadly toward him. A gesture of pity. So there is some reason in her.

It's midday and we've stopped. Sitting like this, I can see treetops over the side of the ship on both right and left. They're close. This is a cove.

I look at the new boys again. They have managed to find each other quickly, even blindfolded. They press together on the deck floor. Their hair is dry. So are their backs. That means this cove is shallow enough to walk in. Even for Brigid.

I lower my head so no one can see where my eyes are directed, and I look up at Brigid. Please, Brigid, look at me, too. Please.

Brigid sits with her back against a wooden chest. Her eyes are closed. But I'm sure she's awake. No one could sleep through that clatter. Besides, it's broad daylight. Why won't she look at me? Why won't she let our eyes talk to each other?

But, oh, she is talking with her eyes. She's saying no. And she's right. Broad daylight is exactly the problem. No chance for escape. Especially with our arms tied. I mustn't be a fool. Picking the right moment is crucial.

The crew members who threw the youths into the boat now climb in. One is Clay Man. The other is almost as tall, with a scar that slants across his forehead and slashes one eyebrow through the center.

We set sail. With our two new prisoners. All children or women. No men. These crew members are not trying to get back at anyone. They're just taking random children and women.

Children and women whisked away. I remember Brogan back in Downpatrick talking of his capture, saying "whisked away." Children and women taken far from home, to lands where we don't even speak the language, where we can be of use only in the most menial tasks.

Oh, Lord.

A hideous guess has been forming in my brain, and now I am entirely sure it is right, for what other answer is there?

This is a slave ship.

CHAPTER TEN:
STORIES

We veer to the right. I stand to see what's going on. We're leaving the coast behind, heading out to open water. The winds are high and the boat goes fast. It's immediately much colder.

Somehow all of us have clustered in the middle of the deck. It's as though an ancient herding instinct has taken over, for I had no intention of coming together with the other prisoners, but here I am.

A slave ship.

Horror seizes me again, and clarifies my vision—with discouraging results. I would wring my hands if they weren't tied. The ten of us are a sorry lot, indeed: the two youths from Saxon Britain, one weeping woman, one crazy woman, the four bleary-eyed children, Brigid, and me. I've seen no evidence one way or another yet whether the youths are competent. But besides them, I am convinced Brigid and I are the most able. We can't count on help from the others. It's up to Brigid and me—it's all up to us. We have to slip away somehow. This cannot happen. Not to us.

HUSH

We sail for a long while. The children and the two youths sink to the deck in a pile. Brigid sinks with them. Soon the weeping woman follows. But the crazy woman and I stay standing.

Ahead all I see is water. I look back. Water. Oh. There's nothing but water in any direction. An eerie feeling creeps through me. In all the ships I've been on, I've never traveled beyond the sight of land. I feel lost. No one can rescue us now. And escape is an illusion.

Oh, Lord. I sink to the deck with the others, unmindful of the pain such careless movement causes. The crazy woman stays standing. I close my eyes. We are in the middle of the sea. We could die. Brigid and I could die on this voyage. I cannot force away the thought: Death could be preferable to the fate ahead. It would be easy to jump overboard and drown.

We Irish are no strangers to drowning. Each settlement knits sweaters in its own unique pattern, so that if a fisherman drowns, when his body washes up on shore he can be returned home. We should be returned home, Brigid and me. It's only right. We should be returned for burial in consecrated ground. This is a degradation a princess must not bear. But if we drowned by our own doing, we wouldn't deserve a Christian burial. We're trapped.

The only consolation is that we're together. *Immalle.*

The wind whistles, and I shiver so hard it makes me tired. I drift in a half sleep.

The crew cheers. I jerk to attention and manage to get to my feet.

There's land to starboard again. That must be why the crew cheered. They've been anxious too. They slap one another on the back and laugh and drink from a beer jug, which almost makes them seem human.

Almost.

The one with a mustache comes around and takes off our gags. He pours beer down our throats. He does this to everyone except the crazy woman. When he turns finally to her, he says something in his incomprehensible language.

She stands there, unblinking.

He takes off her gag.

She shouts, "I will bite. Never fear: I will bite off any part of you that comes near me."

The mustache man steps back, holding the jug. His brow furrows.

The child who fed the woman parsnip before moves in front of her. "I'll give it to her. Just untie my hands." He turns around and extends his hands toward the mustache man. He looks over his shoulder at him. "Please, sir."

The mustache man steps farther back, but his face shows he's trying to understand.

"Please, sir," says the child. "A dead woman is no use to anyone."

I cannot understand how these children speak so sensibly. Such maturity can come only from experience.

"Please," says the weeping woman. "Untie the boy. Let him give her the beer. Please."

The mustache man unties the child's hands. If it had been Clay Man or Leering Man or Club Fist or Scar Face, this wouldn't have happened. I don't know about the rest of the crew, but there's no reason to think they're any better. The crazy woman is lucky today.

The boy holds the jug to the crazy woman's mouth. She drinks as though her thirst will never be slaked. I cannot understand that boy, taking risks like that. For what?

Mustache Man goes toward the bow of the ship, but Clay Man yells at him. He hesitates, then comes back and gags us again.

But he leaves that child's hands untied.

We sail a long while more, always heading north. We skirt along the western coast of some country that can only be described as godforsaken. It's sparsely populated, at least from what can be seen out here on the water. The dwellings are of sod, twigs, clay, and driftwood, and every one of them is small and low. Not a single noble manor house. Not a single church.

We pass a boy leading a cow. Alone. Clay Man shouts something to the crew. My hands clutch at the cloth behind my back.

Moments later our boat drops anchor off a little beach. I pray, despite the fact that I am certain of what is coming.

Scar Face and another crew member—a tall, muscular one with a thick neck that pulses visibly—lower themselves over the side with a splash. The water is so shallow they slog through it to the shore easily.

Clay Man is smart to have made Mustache Man gag us again. I've looked into the eyes of the others by now. They might very well shout warning to that boy and cow if they could. There's a recklessness in them I cannot fathom. But it's not contagious; I will exercise caution to the end. I will take care of Brigid.

The crew members pick animal hide blankets off a pile and throw them around their shoulders. I thought before that the cold came mainly because we were moving. But even now, anchored here, I shiver. We're much farther north than we were this dawn. Shivering makes my rib ache even more deeply. I long to huddle with Brigid under a blanket. Such a small thing, a thing I took for granted only days ago—it's become an unattainable dream.

The two Saxon youths, the ones who wear only trousers, sit hunched over themselves, knees to chest, and visibly shake. One of them eyes that pile of blankets. I watch him. I see the children watching him too.

The child who helped the crazy woman looks at the other children. I thought he helped the crazy woman because she was special to him. His mother, maybe. He ran to her once, after all. But the way he's looking at those youths, I see he wants to help them, too. His eyes shine. The poor thing—why, he's so daft, he would help a total stranger.

I wonder if anyone realized who Saint Patrick truly was while he was still a slave? Are we born to be good or evil? Does daftness help us do the Lord's work?

The boy dashes over and grabs the top hide blanket.

Club Fist lunges. He snatches away the hide and punches the boy on the shoulder. The boy goes flying into the side of the ship. He falls in a crumpled heap.

Weeping Woman screams inside her gag. She sobs so hard, she chokes. Her face turns red. She doubles over.

I look at Brigid. She stares coldly at me. There's nothing we can do.

And for the sake of whatever plan we are to come up

with, we must blend in. This will be our ultimate salvation. If we are to have one.

Mustache Man walks across the deck. He lifts the
small, limp child, who in my head I hereby dub Patrick
after our patron saint, and lays him on a blanket. We
stare as he folds the sides onto the boy's chest.

One of the Saxon youths gets stiffly to his feet. He
goes to stand in front of Mustache Man. His whole body
trembles with cold. His torso has a slight blue-gray tinge.

Mustache Man just looks at him.

The other Saxon youth comes forward too. A pitiful
pair.

Mustache Man opens a chest and takes out a shirt.
He goes to another chest and takes out a second shirt. He
unties the youths' hands and gives them the shirts.

We stare and stare, caught in the spell of inexplicable
kindness.

Clay Man comes suddenly alive. He barks something
at Club Fist. Club Fist rushes over and snatches the
shirts back from the youths. He reties their hands tight
at their backs. Clay Man stomps to the boy Patrick and
rips the blanket away. The boy slides off, a clutter of
limbs.

Clay Man glares at Mustache Man, who now sits on
his chest without a word.

Two of the children go kneel by the limp child, my sweet Patrick. Patrick opens his eyes and stares at the sky.

The rest of us mill around now. The show is over, and it helps to move; it stirs our innards to fan whatever embers might still glow.

I think about home; that helps me to stay warm too. Mother, Father, Nuada. But my mind has less urgency now. The cold dampers everything except the need to get warm.

And maybe it isn't just the cold that dampers me. A terrible and unavoidable thought slows my brain. Brigid and I are farther away with each passing moment. Even if we do manage to escape, we might never make it back to Eire. We may never know what happened at Downpatrick the night Bjarni came. This thought is almost unbearable. I want to slam my head against the mast and make it go away. I will not let our lives be truncated. I will not allow that first part to be lost. All the people, all the places we ever loved.

My belly twists inside with a dull heavy hurt that presses down. Nausea rises. My head spins. I recognize this feeling. My monthly blood is coming.

Club Fist calls something. Someone answers from beyond the ship. A boy falls onto the deck with a wet thud. He scrambles to his feet as Scar Face and the other crew member climb in behind him. Scar Face knocks the boy down. The poor boy with the cow. The poor lost child.

We leave, sailing fast into the ice air. We're far from land in no time at all. After a while Clay Man shouts. The crew lower the sails, then herd us prisoners toward the aft of the ship, even little Patrick, who has to be half carried, and hem us in. Their bodies form a fence. All except Weeping Woman. She's left out.

What's going on? I look back at her. Her eyes grow frantic. She runs to join us, but crew members block her way.

The Saxon youths exchange glances, then throw themselves as one against the crew. They are beaten down. Rolled onto their sides. Kicked.

Of course. Their arms are bound. What could they do but throw themselves like sacks of dirt?

Clay Man grabs Weeping Woman. He pushes her to the deck. He tugs up her tunic.

I fight back tears and take small steps and try to cluster the children together with little bumps of my knees. Crazy Woman and Brigid do the same. We huddle together and move the children to the very tip of the boat so that we three and the battered youths form a layer between the children and the fence of crew members.

HUSH

We can hear the scuffle behind us. The boy with the cow turns to look, but I knock him hard with one knee and he quickly faces the tip of the boat again. I will let none of them see this.

For the first time I'm grateful for these gags. The woman must be screaming inside her head, but the sound doesn't reach us. The children don't know.

And I won't look at Brigid. I won't let her read in my eyes what she might not be sure of on her own.

But my eyes meet Crazy Woman's eyes. And I see an iron will. No, she's not crazy at all. She bit Club Fist for precisely this reason. To let them all know she'll fight like a wildcat. To make them decide she's more trouble than she's worth. A lost parsnip was a simple price to pay to save her from this.

If I were thrown to the floor like Weeping Woman, my cracked rib could snap and pierce my heart.

I'd want it to.

Clay Man says something. I look over my shoulder. He's changing places with Leering Man. They're taking turns. One offense after the other.

Something inside me breaks. I twist my torso to face them and shake my head no.

Clay Man stares at me with surprise on his face.

I'm surprised too. I recognize the futility, but I

cannot stop. My head shakes so hard, I think it will fly off. Shame on you, I scream inside my head. Shame!

Someone nearby kicks me. It could only be Crazy Woman. She's right; sense returns.

I face aft again and huddle over the children. The crew are still at it. Will there be anything left of Weeping Woman? I squeeze my eyes hard against tears. My nose flares with pent-up misery. But I will not shed a single drop. Boys don't cry.

Night finally comes. It's freezing. Spring was easing into Eire, but here, as we head north, it's like we're going backward in time. It's cold as winter. The wind cuts my face.

After the assault on Weeping Woman, the crew members went to the oars and rowed, even though the sails were up once more. They rowed as though there was no time to waste, without even feeding us. The prisoners have fallen asleep in little clusters. Including Brigid. I look at her with dismay; we're becoming one with the rest of them—all equally pathetic.

Well, I will not sleep, not me. I watch everything. I will learn the crew's habits. I will pick out their weaknesses. I will find a way to get Brigid and me free.

Clay Man lights an oil lamp and sets it on the deck. I'm surprised. They didn't use a lamp last night. It gives off a rancid smoke, nothing like the sweet burn of fat-dipped reeds and rushes back home, and a world different from the clean burn of wax candles at a holiday meal.

Thick Neck comes around waking us and untying our hands. It looks like we're going to eat, after all. Three men stand with spears at the ready—Club Fist and Leering Man and a third, darker-skinned and gray-haired, with the regal bearing of our great Irish hounds used in hunting elk and wolves. I dub him Wolf Hound. They guard us particularly well right now.

And they're feeding us differently. Mustache Man unties the gag of one child, hands him a lump of dried bread and a piece of salted fish, and waits till he finishes eating. Then he regags the child and ungags the next one, but only for as long as it takes that child to eat. Now he's ungagging the third child.

I see why. The boat has turned. We're going up a river. Four of the crew are at the oars and one is at the tiller. The river is wide and we stay in the center. But there must be scattered settlements on either side. If we shouted together now, all of us prisoners, we might have a chance at waking the people out there. But if only one of us is ungagged at a time, if only one of us shouts, who can hear? Especially since we'll be beaten into submission immediately.

We could untie our own gags. Our hands are free.

But would it really do any good? If I lifted my hands to untie my gag, Club Fist would surely strike me down.

After all, they must defend their cargo.

We're their cargo.

I hang my hands dead at my sides.

In the glow of the lamp, they are colorless. I wiggle the fingers. That hurts.

And my lips are chapped.

When I was standing by the ropes before, my head hung to one side, I was so tired. Frost formed on the shoulder of my tunic where my breath hit it. We need blankets or we're all going to get sick. And these children are skin and bones. Underfed to start with. They'll die. But what can I do? What can any of us do?

When it's finally my turn to eat and they ungag me, I wolf down my fish and gnaw greedily at my bread. I am as useless as everyone else here. The fine Princess Melkorka. What a joke. My colorless hands shake.

Crazy Woman is eating now. But when it comes time to regag her, she snaps her head around and spits and hisses like a mad thing. She pushes her way into the center of the prisoners. "Come listen," she calls. "Story time. Picture two men. No, no, they aren't your father. They aren't your big brother or your husband or any one of these devil crew members. These are men you've never seen before.

"Let your eyes follow my words and paint them. They are very much alike in body. Almost twins. Strong, with arms that can haul in nets so teeming with fish that but five loads would fill this ship. And backs and legs so powerful that they can run through forests carrying whole felled trees on their shoulders. The one goes by the name Aedan, the other by the name Calhoun."

I don't recognize the names. Crazy Woman is making up this story. But what does it matter? We circle her, moving in close. The boy who led the cow appears rapt—though his language is anyone's guess. Even the Saxon youths listen, and I'm sure they don't understand Gaelic.

To my surprise, Clay Man allows it. Maybe he even thinks it's a good thing—it will keep us occupied as we travel this river with sleepers out there in the dark on both sides.

"But though they look like twins outside," says Crazy Woman, "inside they are completely different. The one called Aedan has always been a servant. He takes orders from the chief, the chief's wife, the chief's son, the chief's daughter, even the chief's baby. He jumps when the chief's dog barks. He walks and eats with his eyes cast down. He wears white.

"Calhoun, though, he's always lived on his own. He

has his own plot of land. He tills and sows and reaps it himself. He bows to no one. If a dog barks at him, he strangles it." Crazy Woman lets her words hang in the air.

Snows begins. It's so light, it floats down rather than falling.

"Calhoun wears a red tunic. Red, you're thinking. What good Irish man wears red? A man who isn't afraid of spirits, that's who. A man who is afraid of nothing. Not even devils. Calhoun tramps everywhere he goes.

"Now one day, Aedan is sent to the forest to fell a tree, and he meets Calhoun."

A single hoot threads through the air.

"*Brid*," says one of the British youths, tapping the shoulder of the other.

What? Is he mispronouncing Brigid's name? How did he learn her name?

But now the other youth lifts his head and cocks an ear toward where the hoot came from. He murmurs, "*Brid*." It must be their word for bird.

"Aedan draws back, of course, yielding the narrow forest path to Calhoun."

The snow softly whitens the youths' hair. It's as though they are fading away. Everything is fading.

Except Crazy Woman. Her voice jumps out from the delicate sweetness of the new snow, all robust and hearty.

She's good at this. I think of my dear Nuada and I have to swallow and swallow, so I won't cry.

"Calhoun sizes up this humble man, who is, in fact, exactly his own size. He points to a giant pine and says, 'I can chop down that tree in the time it takes you to count to ten and carry it on the back of my neck to the river before you can reach twenty-five.'

"Aedan believes him, of course, because Aedan could do the same. Aedan nods.

"'Are you saying you're not surprised?' asks Calhoun. 'You should be so surprised, you soil your small-clothes.'"

A child laughs, muffled in his gag.

"'Why should I be surprised?' says Aedan in a gentle voice. 'I could do the same.'

"'You? You're too tiny,' says Calhoun.

"Aedan does not take offense at being called tiny. He doesn't realize his own strength and size.

"'You're a liar,' adds Calhoun.

"Being called a liar, well, that's another thing entirely. Aedan never lies. He shakes his head.

"'Is that denial?' asks Calhoun. 'That mincy, girly little nod? Are you going to do a curtsy, too?'"

Now all the children laugh. All but Brigid and the boy who led the cow.

"Calhoun shakes his head in disgust. 'I suppose we'll have to battle over that.'

"For four days, the two men battle. Imagine it. Ah, but you're imagining wrong. Calhoun may be as fierce as an animal, but still he is a man. He has honor. So they fight fairly, both of them.

"They alternate who picks the weapons. The first day Calhoun chooses darts. He is superb at darts. He wins.

"The second day Aedan chooses stabbing spears. He is superb at stabbing spears. He wins. But each day," says Crazy Woman, "one wins by only a tiny bit, because they are equal in abilities. They are almost twins. Like I said. It's just that Calhoun knows who he is and Aedan doesn't. Calhoun has always had his freedom, but Aedan needs to learn to seize his.

"At the end of that day they hug and kiss, as warriors should do. Are you surprised I called them warriors? This peasant and this servant? That's what they are. That's what we all are. Warriors in life.

"The third day they duel with broadswords. That's Calhoun's choice, for it's his turn again. Do you know who wins?" asks Crazy Woman.

The child who laughed earlier nods. Another child nods too. And Patrick nods.

"Calhoun has to win," says Crazy Woman. "Right?"

All four Irish children nod. Brigid nods.

"He's superb at broadswords. That's why he chose them."

Darts, stabbing spears, broadswords . . . Oh, I recognize this series. Warriors, indeed.

"On the fourth day Aedan chooses . . ."

Ford combat, I say inside my head.

". . . ford combat," says Crazy Woman.

This is a well-known tale, after all; it's Cúchulainn and Ferdia's battle. Aedan will win. And he will kill Calhoun. Why is Crazy Woman disguising the tale?

"Strong arms count in the water," says Crazy Woman. "Strong, strong arms."

I feel eyes on me. I look around.

It's Brigid. Her eyes are bright. She jerks her head once, then runs and jumps up and over the side of the ship. Before I can react, one of the youths jumps after her.

Of course. Our arms are free still. We can swim. Like ford combat. I run, but too late. Clay Man grabs me around the waist. He shouts. Crew members surround the rest of the prisoners. Club Fist holds a spear and throws it into the night, into the void that swallowed Brigid and the youth. He picks up another spear. Can he see in this darkness?

I desperately tug on the string that hangs around my

neck. Stork feathers fly from my bodice along with the pouch, and I'm shaking that pouch insistently in front of Clay Man's eyes and biting down so hard on the gag that I think my teeth will tear through it and break on each other.

Clay Man grabs the pouch, drops me, and yanks it off over my head. I turn to run again but instantly Clay Man shouts, and Club Fist puts down the spear and pushes me into the circle of prisoners.

Clay Man squats by the lamp and rolls the precious ring over and over in his hand. My gold teething ring that Father gave me at my birth, that Mother so sagely tucked in that pouch. He picks up the three stork feathers and holds them to his lips. "*Aist*," he says, beating out two syllables loudly: a-ist. He looks up at me with wonder on his face. Snowflakes sit on his eyebrows.

Brigid is gone.

Clay Man stares at me. "*Aist*."

I am alone. And Brigid is out there in the freezing water.

I fall on my knees and press my forehead against the deck.

CHAPTER ELEVEN:
HUSH

A hide blanket comes down over my back. I look up at Clay Man. He's a watery blur through my misery.

Brigid is gone.

Clay Man says something in a quiet voice. I jump away.

He jumps too, as though for an instant he thought I might attack him. He speaks again. An ugly, stupid language. An ugly, stupid man.

He backs away from me slowly, rolling the ring in one hand, clutching the three stork feathers in the other. He says something to the crew members.

They return to their posts. Rowing, rowing. All but Thick Neck. He picks up the oil lamp and comes over near me, lamp on high. I am illuminated in the silent snow that keeps falling, soft as mouse breath.

I move out of the glow.

Clay Man says something.

Thick Neck backs away.

Every few moments Clay Man looks at me. His eyes

glisten, but his face is too much in the dark and too far away to be readable.

The children look at me too. From close by. And their faces speak clearly: envy.

I take the blanket from my shoulders and drape it over the children. They lie down and squirm together like the piglets Brigid put ribbons on her last day in Downpatrick. Four Irish babes and one boy who led a cow. The blanket is big, and they are little. There's enough to tuck them in at the edges.

And what do I care about being warm? Brigid is gone.

I look back at Clay Man. He frowns. Even from here distress is unmistakable. He walks over to the blanket pile and goes to put a second one on me.

But I grab it from his hand before he can touch me. I shake with fear.

He makes a quick intake of breath. Then he backs away again. The three stork feathers are still in one hand. I don't see where he put the ring.

I give the blanket to Crazy Woman. She doesn't hesitate. She beckons over Weeping Woman and the still bare-chested Saxon youth who stayed behind. The three of them immediately lie close together under the second blanket.

Clay Man stares at me.

I stare back. Brigid is gone. Nothing matters. I shiver. My teeth chatter.

Crazy Woman lifts the edge of the blanket. Her eyes are barely visible in the lamplight. Still, they command. And I know I should obey, though I've forgotten why. I wiggle myself in beside her. We are not small, so the blanket is hardly adequate for four. Crazy Woman should have left me standing. I close my eyes.

+ + +

I wake. I eat. I use the pot. I sleep.

Days go by. I'm not sure how many.

I go long stretches without thinking. But when I do think, it feels unreal. Brigid cannot have jumped overboard. I cannot still be on this ship.

I sit by the mast and bleed onto my tunic. I don't care what a mess I make of myself. I wish all my blood would come out and drown Clay Man. And Leering Man. And Club Fist. And all of them. All of them are complicit.

None of them comes near me except at mealtimes.

Our gags come off to eat. The others talk. I don't. And I don't listen, either.

Life is a blur.

✦   ✦   ✦

One morning I wake and look around and my eyes actually function. The boat is not moving. We must be anchored.

Clay Man wears my teething ring on a leather strap around his neck. The three stork feathers are jammed in his hair at odd angles.

I had forgotten all about those feathers. They were supposed to be a surprise for Brigid, to lift her spirits when times got hard. How naive I was—I never imagined anything as hard as what has happened.

Crazy Woman's eyes meet mine. Hers light up. She comes over and sits beside me and whispers in my ear, "I'm Maeve."

I cannot respond. She's the only one not wearing a gag. Did Clay Man never have it put back on her after the night she told stories? The night Brigid left. My own gag is gummy in my mouth. And it stinks.

Maeve kisses my cheek. "That's Gormlaith." She tilts her head toward Weeping Woman. "She gave me her name last night. At the evening meal."

Maeve and Gormlaith. Good Gaelic names. I look at the youth from Saxon Britain.

Maeve's eyes follow mine. "He's William. He doesn't speak Gaelic. But he can say his name, at least."

William is sitting with one of the children on his lap. He's playing some sort of hand-clapping game. His breath makes smoke in the air. The child's head bends toward that smoke.

"The boy we picked up in Saxland is called Markus. The Irish boys are Morc and Nyle. The girls are Kacey and Riley."

Markus I can pick out—he's the one who led the cow. But for the Irish children, I wonder which ones go with which names. I will continue to call the child who helps everyone Patrick, even if he turns out to be a girl.

"We have a name for you," says Maeve.

I already have a name. But that doesn't matter so much. I move my face toward her curiously.

"Aist."

I flinch. I remember Clay Man repeating that word the night Brigid left.

"Ah, so you recognize it," says Maeve. "It's Russian. Adopt it and you'll be saved." She stands up. "Now, shall we clean you?"

Saved? The word has little meaning.

Maeve pulls me up by the hand. Our hands are free. Have they been since the night Brigid left?

She leads me to a wide bucket of water. It's iced over on top. I realize I'm shivering.

I look over the ship's side.

We're near a shore to our right. A sandy beach stretches far inland toward towering trees. Sunlight shimmers on the frost in the highest needles of the evergreens. A small cove lies ahead. The little lagoon within it is ice-covered. Ice on salt water. We must be very far north if there's ice in the sea so late as March.

"Don't look too long," says Maeve. "It will discourage you. The Russians call this the Baltic. It's the East Sea. A strange sea. Here." She breaks the ice in the bucket with her fist. It doesn't crack; it slushes apart. She scoops with a cupped hand and brings water to my mouth. "Taste. Put your head back and I'll dribble it over your gag."

Maybe she is crazy.

But I do as she says. The water soaks through and around my gag. It is foul, but that may be my own sour tastes.

"See? It's hardly salty."

That's true. The Irish Sea is much stronger.

Some of the crew are watching now. Leering Man, Club Fist, Thick Neck, and, of course, Clay Man. He's always watching me. Two others, the ones who seem to have nothing to do with us prisoners, are playing a game with what look like colored pebbles. And some crew members are missing. Three?

"Gormlaith," calls Maeve, "come help."

Gormlaith's face is drawn. Her hair stands out like a wild thing's. She favors her right side as she approaches. She moves like an old woman. But I know she's not. I remember how she was when I first saw her.

William and the children watch.

"Treat her like you'd like to be treated," says Maeve in a scolding tone.

The Irish children go to the front of the boat. William and Markus follow. They sit as a group, their backs to us, a blanket stretched across them.

Maeve and Gormlaith stand on either side of me and pull my tunic up.

I fight to hold it down. I look around at the crew.

"Forget their eyes," says Maeve. "They're animals."

That's exactly my fear. I sink to my haunches and hold the hem of my tunic to the deck and I realize that my rib doesn't hurt nearly so bad now. The body heals on its own—perhaps in spite.

"They won't touch you," says Maeve. "They won't dare. Not with him looking on. Not with what he believes." She jerks her chin toward Clay Man. "And you'll get sores and fever and delirium if you don't clean up." She beckons. "Nyle, come help."

Nyle turns out to be my Patrick. He comes running.

"Stand wherever you can to block the view of her. You'll have to change positions as we move. Just do the best you can."

Again Maeve and Gormlaith reach for my tunic.

I close my eyes.

When Nuada was little, we'd play hide-and-seek. I was two years older than him, and I won. But, in fact, anyone could hide better than Nuada. He didn't go behind anything. He simply closed his eyes, believing that if he couldn't see you, you couldn't see him. Once he finally figured things out, the game was no longer fun. He was quick and quiet and he won all the time.

I open my eyes and force myself to lift my arms over my head.

They pull off my tunic and sink it into the bucket water. Then Maeve lightly slaps my own sopping tunic on my belly.

The shock of the freezing water makes me jump.

Brigid jumped into freezing water. As snow fell.

They scrub me with that dirty tunic. They scrub me everywhere. I turn under their hands like I did under Delaney's hands the night we rushed back from Dublin, when Nuada's hand was cut off.

They scrub my face. They wash my hair.

I shiver violently. My jaw tries to chatter. I taste blood

as the corners of my mouth rip on the crusty edges of the gag.

They wrap me in the second blanket.

"Now you," says Maeve to Gormlaith.

Gormlaith takes the wet tunic and washes her face and hands and feet.

Maeve nods to my Patrick.

He washes obediently.

"Come for a wash," calls Maeve.

All the others scrub themselves with my dirty tunic, Maeve last of all.

Then she scrubs my tunic in the bucket and stretches it over a chest to dry.

She dumps the brown, filthy water over the side of the ship. Then she lowers the bucket by the attached string and brings it back up full again. And the water is brown again. It wasn't my filth that made it that color.

This is a brackish sea. With hardly any salt. How strange everything is here. Nothing is as it seems.

Maeve comes over and snakes her hand inside the blanket and pinches me hard.

I gasp.

"You are right to keep your voice to yourself, Aist," she says into my ear. "Hush. You're the one who started this silence—you have to keep it up. Or you lose yourself.

He'll just snuff you out." She makes a puff of hot air that warms my brain. "Like that, like a lamp flame. A slave life counts for nothing unless the slave finds a trick. You've found yours. Stick to it. Hush."

I don't understand. But I will hold my tongue. The last person who told me to hush was Mother.

+ + +

Travel is slow. We pass rivers that empty into this sea. Many. That must be why this water is so nearly sweet. But I have no explanation for why it is so brackish.

At the mouth of almost every river, we stop and anchor nearby. The crew take turns going ashore—two or three at a time. They bring back barrels of fresh water. They bring back river fish. They bring back game that they roast on the beach. They bring back jugs of beer, though where the people are that they get that beer from, I do not know.

They share it all with us. The first time we feasted, Maeve mumbled to me, "They're fattening us up. There must be a slave market ahead within a half moon at the most. Otherwise they'd never do this. Fat slaves bring more money than skinny ones, because they don't drop dead on you right off." The very next day Clay Man finally gave a shirt to William. Maeve hissed in my ear, "So he'll be warm enough to put on a little flesh. Hogs before the slaughter, that's what we are." Clay Man pinches the upper arms of the children each morning, clearly measuring their fat with his fingers. Sometimes we eat so much, I think my belly will split.

It is bitterly cold. Each morning I wake with dread that a child will have succumbed to the chill overnight. No one does. Somehow the abundant food sustains us, down to the weakest, who is Kacey.

I spend daytime standing as close to the shore side of the deck as I can get. I watch the land.

It's been twelve days since I started counting. And I started counting the day Maeve washed me.

I stand and watch the land and see four children. Out in the open. Like flowers waiting to be plucked.

Clay Man's shout interrupts my thought. I wince. He must be constantly scanning for prey to be so quick about it. A serious predator.

As soon as we have passed the next curve of shore and are out of the children's sight line, we drop anchor. Of course.

My head spins.

Five men hold spears pointed at us.

Four men go over the side of the boat and run back along the beach. Four. One per child.

Oh so soon, they are back, carrying trussed children on their shoulders, like sacks of meal.

These children fight less than Markus or William did. They fight less than Brigid and I did. Maybe that's because Clay Man talks to them as they are dumped into the ship. They appear to understand his language. At least somewhat. He says things and they act as a unit, clearly following directions.

By nightfall their obedience has so mollified Clay Man that he has their blindfolds removed and hands untied. But they stay gagged like the rest of us—except for Maeve.

We eat. As the gags come off, people talk to one another. Even William and Markus join the talk, though no one else speaks the language of either one of them.

Maeve sits beside me. She barely moves her lips as she speaks softly. "Silence, Aist. It will pay off in the end. You're smart enough, I can tell." And she pinches me hard enough to bring tears.

I didn't need the reminder. "Hush" has become my internal chant. It drums in Mother's voice like a heartbeat. I eat with my gaze lowered.

Then we are gagged again. Except for Maeve.

Night comes. We move into a circle around Maeve. She calms us with stories. Tonight's story is of the gods. Last night's was of the heroes. She alternates. They aren't in disguise anymore; they are our traditional Irish tales. I look forward to them.

Riley climbs onto my lap. This has become her habit. I am almost sure that Morc and Kasey are brother and sister. And maybe Patrick-Nyle is their brother too. They are far enough apart in age for that to be possible. But Riley seems to be alone on this ship, and she latches on to me at storytime.

The four new children listen, rapt. Though they cannot understand the words, somehow they under-stand that these are stories. Somehow they enjoy them.

As Maeve talks I grow rapt as well. But in a different way. I ride a current of fantasy. This is not Maeve who speaks. This is Nuada. We are not on this Russian slave ship. We are in Downpatrick. The child on my lap is not Riley, but Brigid.

And I am not Aist. I am, once more, Melkorka.

This current is wonderful.

When Maeve finally stops, the Irish children and Markus pile together under a blanket. Maeve and Gormlaith and William pile under our other blanket.

I watch the four new children.

Their clothing is warmer than ours. But I cannot ignore the fact that the night wind off the water stabs like an ice pick.

I go over to the crew's pile of blankets and take a third one.

Clay Man rushes over. I knew he would. I knew he was watching me. He's always watching me. I hear his clumping feet.

I spin around to face him, to meet his blow head-on.

He shouts at me.

But I am still in the haze of Maeve's storytelling. I am still Melkorka, the princess of Downpatrick. If I didn't have this gag on, I would shout back. I rip at the gag.

His eyes open wider. He appears enormously surprised. He grabs my arm and turns me around and works at the knot on my gag. He's going to unleash my tongue himself. He wants me to shout at him.

The gag comes away.

"Aist," shouts Maeve. "Aist."

"Aist?" says Clay Man. It's a question.

Hush, says Mother inside my head.

I face Clay Man.

"Aist?" he asks.

I walk past him, clutching the blanket to my chest. I give it to the tallest of the new children.

The new children lie down together in a pile under the third blanket.

I go over to Maeve and nestle in beside her, and I

realize that the movement brings only a muted, distant hurt, almost the memory of pain rather than the thing itself. My bones grow strong again.

"You did good," she says in my ear. "The children from Vendland will sleep. You did good. You sleep now too, Aist."

Maeve knows that the land we picked those children up in is called Vendland. Maeve knows a lot. This fact comforts me.

CHAPTER TWELVE: THE VOW

Freezing rain thumps on the blankets that we hold overlapping above our heads like a tent. The rain's so solid, it bounces on the deck. It cuts the backs of my hands where I clutch blanket. It darkens this midday to almost night.

Maeve and Gormlaith and William and I are the pillars of the blanket tent. Nine children crowd underneath, pressed so close together, it's a wonder they can breathe. The fronts of our bodies are under the blankets too, but our backs receive the pelting rain. I feel oddly euphoric. My body shields these children. It is a small thing, but it's mine, and it makes me glad.

A child manages to squirm around and grasp Maeve around the waist. It's Morc.

As the rain finally eases a little, Maeve sings to him. It's a lullaby about a baby named Ula. Maeve puts in Morc's name instead.

The children sway to the tune. It's so hideously cold, but they sway as though everything is normal, life is how it should be. My heart applauds them.

Now Maeve sings the song again, but she puts in Kacey's name. Then Nyle's—my Patrick. Then Riley's. Then Markus's.

But she doesn't put in the names of the four new children. The ones who were stolen yesterday. We don't know their names. When we ate this morning, those children sat silent. The gloom of a new slave.

I stare down at the top of the head of the child pressing against my chest. This poor soul. He needs a lullaby too. Even if his ears don't know what the Gaelic words mean, he can take courage from the sound of his own name. Markus certainly doesn't understand, yet he turned his head toward Maeve when he heard his name. He looked at her with all the naked need to be cared for that children have. The new children should have a lullaby too.

My cold-stiffened fists tighten on the blanket edge painfully. The rain gradually stops. I'm still shaking.

The crew members crawl out from under their own blankets. They hoist the sails again and man the oars. Mustache Man and Thick Neck hang the crew's blankets from the lower parts of the masts to dry.

William carries our blankets over to hang them, too. Thick Neck yells at him. But our blankets have to dry. Otherwise we'll freeze tonight.

William attaches one blanket to the mast.

Thick Neck punches him in the back, knocking him to the deck.

I race over and pull him up by the elbow.

Thick Neck yells at me and the vessels in his neck stand out like ropes.

Clay Man comes barreling over, shouting. I close my eyes and brace for a blow. But he's shouting at Thick Neck, not at me.

And somehow I'm not really surprised. Somehow I knew that blow wouldn't come.

I let go of William and attach our second blanket. And then the third blanket. I feel Clay Man's eyes on me. I don't look at him.

I walk over to one of the new children. Clay Man's eyes bore through me. I untie his gag. It's slow, because the knot is truly complicated. And it's damp. But I get it off and I throw it over the side of the boat.

Many eyes are on me now. I see them peripherally.

I walk to another of the new children and untie his, too. And throw it away.

Leering Man pulls in his oar and shouts. Club Fist shouts as well. Then Leering Man gets up and comes toward me, screaming.

Clay Man moves between Leering Man and me. They argue. Clay Man puffs out his chest. His hands close into rocks. And I remember what Maeve said when she was trying to get me to take off my tunic so she could wash me. This crew won't dare touch me with Clay Man looking on.

He protects me. How far, I wonder. I'm already untying the gag of the third new child. Then the fourth.

Now I turn to the Irish children. Patrick-Nyle first. But his gag is much harder to undo, because it's much filthier. I don't see how the crew can undo it so quickly at meal times. They should thank me for getting rid of these gags; it's one less chore for them.

And, really, who are we going to shout to out here? Even if we saw people, how could they help us? It would take a dozen men to overcome this ship. A small army. It doesn't matter if we wear these gags or not. It matters only to us. Perhaps they will see this reason. Perhaps I will not pay for my actions.

I untie Morc's gag, and Patrick-Nyle unties Kacey's gag.

Club Fist runs at Patrick-Nyle. He's the one who hurt Patrick-Nyle before.

I fly between them.

And Club Fist winds up sending me careening across the slippery deck—*crack*—into the corner of a chest. My tunic goes instantly red at the shoulder. The dull ache of my broken rib now turns to a knife stab again. Even the slight movement of breath hurts.

All I can think is that I was wrong; every action costs.

Clay Man and Club Fist shout at each other. I watch them from the floor of the deck. My powerlessness over what is to happen next gives me a heady clarity. We are flimsy people compared to this crew. But they are remarkably stupid. They go through all this trouble to steal us and fatten us up, but they can't sell us if we're dead. That's what Patrick-Nyle tried to point out to Mustache Man back when they were starving Maeve. How is it that dunces become masters and children as bright as Patrick-Nyle become slaves?

Clay Man shakes my gold teething ring at Club Fist. He touches the feathers on his head. The word "*aist*" comes up often in his shouts.

Club Fist looks at me suspiciously and backs off.

Clay Man picks up Morc's gag where I dropped it and dips it into the bucket of seawater we always have available. He comes toward me.

I raise my hand to stop him. A pathetic gesture, hardly more than the breath before a prayer.

And he stops. That huge man stops.

Clay Man holds out the wet rag to Patrick-Nyle and says something.

"What do I do?" sobs Patrick-Nyle.

"Come to me," says Maeve.

He runs and buries his head in her belly.

Clay Man calls over one of the new children. He says something.

The child comes to me and bathes my bleeding shoulder with the wet gag.

Clay Man admonishes, and the child touches me more gently.

Clay Man's face softens. He comes toward me slowly, walking as if balancing on the top of a narrow wall.

I try to get to my feet, but pain stops me.

He gets on one knee and turns my head toward him. He whispers something. It feels like a question. He wants an answer.

Many tongues are free now. These children control so little, but they are the masters of what they say, at least. And that's my doing. I restored that right.

And I am the master of what I say. Clay Man can ask whatever he wants, however many times he wants. But all I listen to is the hush, from deep inside me.

I hold my tongue.

✦   ✦   ✦

A few days later the landscape changes. Low hills roll as far as I can see. They make it seem as though the ground is waking up. The air loses its sharp edge. It feels and looks more like my own Eire. Spring is coming, even to this north place.

And, ironically, Thick Neck coughs, deep and phlegmy. He started two nights ago and it's clear that he has caught a sickness. But we prisoners breathe freely.

Our ship sails farther from shore than before. I believe this is Clay Man's way of controlling the crew's anxiety over the fact that all of us are ungagged now. When we woke up the morning after I had untied so many gags, all the rest were gone. The crew had a little meeting, then the ship veered out into the water more. Irish words speckle the air all day long now, and it hardly matters that no one on shore hears them, for we hear them. Blessèd Irish words.

It's mealtime. The prisoners move into a circle. I bend and put one hand on the deck and lower myself to sitting, careful not to jostle the scab covering the wound on my shoulder. It is impossible not to hurt my ribs, so I simply breathe deeply through every movement, bearing that pain as best I can.

The children who can speak with Clay Man—the ones Maeve calls Slavs—serve us our fish. Their names are Boleslaw, Tabor, Obdor, and Padnik. I believe they are all boys.

Everyone else is talking. Even William and Markus do a reasonable job of making themselves understood through gestures. Morc eagerly teaches them words. The simple act of gabbing unites us. My dead tongue twitches in a hint of longing.

As Obdor gets to me, he looks over his shoulder at Clay Man. Then he skips me. I stare at Clay Man. He regards me with a close-lipped smile. I would take a fish myself, but Obdor and his basket are already out of reach.

Everyone has been served. Everyone eats.

Padnik comes around with the beer jug. He skips me.

I don't know why I'm being punished. Since the day I untied gags, I have done nothing but stay as immobile as possible. All I want to do is heal.

My stomach squeezes hard on its emptiness. I look down and clench my teeth. I hurt too much for any action.

Shoes appear before me. I look up at Clay Man. He holds a fish. He squats and dangles it in front of me.

I grab for it. He quickly pulls it back out of reach. He says something and points toward my mouth.

I am hungry. He knows that. I open my mouth to show him.

He dangles the fish again. And I realize what he

wants: for me to talk. That's what this is all about. It bothers him that I don't speak. That very fact alone is enough to make me hold my tongue.

I stare through him.

The day is long. I do not stand to watch the shore. I try to sleep.

Clay Man repeats the routine at the evening meal. This time the fish he dangles is bigger than the fish the others got. He is determined. His voice is actually sweet, sticky sweet. He holds the fish close enough for me to smell. But it's the beer I want more than the fish. I'm so thirsty. I remember how Maeve didn't eat and didn't drink. I stare through him.

In the morning Boleslaw serves the fish. He skips me. And Padnik skips me on the beer.

I remember when Maeve whispered in my ear that a slave's life counts for nothing without a trick. Silence was my trick. But this has gone way beyond a trick. My insides burn constantly. My vision blurs. I fear walking for dizziness. The trick is on me.

Clay Man talks to me. He eats a fish in front of me, chewing big. Revulsion makes me contract, my chest on my knees, my arms closed around my shins.

And this evening Tabor skips me on the fish, and Obdor skips me on the beer.

Clay Man talks to me. He eats slowly, his face close to mine. He looks at my face and he stares into my eyes.

I care very much about that food. But it is no longer hard to pretend I don't, for now I'm very tired. I do not stare through him. Rather, I close my eyes. My thoughts move as slowly as my eyelids. I didn't know I could be this stubborn. Brigid is the one Mother always called stubborn. Me she called rash.

I am doing this now in Brigid's honor, I suppose. Yes, Brigid is the very definition of stubbornness. Indeed, my silence has now become a vow.

At least my mouth no longer fills with saliva at the sight of food. I am totally dry. And I can't even smell the fish or beer anymore. The world closes itself off from me.

It seems I'm going deaf, too, deaf as well as mute. For the only thing I can hear is coughing. Thick Neck, undoubtedly. Coughing and gagging. I fall asleep to coughing.

In the morning I get no fish, no beer. I sleep poorly most of the day. Thick Neck sleeps near me. He shakes from fever. It takes all my energy to turn my head away from him. At night Obdor passes me by with the fish basket. I see him and I don't care. I cough weakly.

Clay Man jumps at my cough and rushes to me. He talks quickly. He looks almost scared. He grabs a fish and pinches off a tiny bit and puts it into my mouth. He slowly feeds me. I let him, though I feel distant, an observer of a scene that has nothing to do with me. He holds the beer jug to my lips as I drink. It sears my throat. My stomach clenches. I vomit. Clay Man moans and feeds me again, more slowly now. And I drink. He croons—that big beast croons. I am stunningly dizzy. But I am back.

It's over. And I won. This time.

◆　◆　◆

Thick Neck disappeared overnight. I stare at the spot he lay those many days. I see others look at it, then glance away. He must have died, and the crew must have thrown him to the fish. I slept too hard after last night's meal to wake for anything.

The crew are jittery. But no one appears sad.

There are now eight of them and thirteen of us.

◆　◆　◆

It is four days since Thick Neck disappeared. We are anchored in a cove. We've been here for three days. The crew have been taking turns guarding us and going ashore. Right now Wolf Hound and Mustache Man climb on board. They haul the carcass of a deer they just roasted on the beach. The smell intoxicates me.

There is something wonderful about meat in the middle of the sea. This is the third day in a row we bite down into flesh. We eat with gusto. The atmosphere is almost festive.

Maeve kisses me on the cheek and speaks softly into my ear. "We all know."

I pull back and blink my eyes questioningly at her.

She smiles and leans in. "For this one moment," she whispers, "it doesn't matter why they fatten us. Feel the magic, Aist? Right now, can you feel it? We are a family."

And I do feel it. I snuggle closer to her.

"I've seen it before. Slavery has a way of foiling itself." She picks a string of venison from between her teeth. "Temporarily, at least."

✦ ✦ ✦

Yesterday my blood came again. I stopped counting the days, but my body does a count of its own. Maeve bleeds too. She started a day before me. There is little privacy on this ship.

I lie awake in the predawn and know I should get

up and clean myself, but I want to sleep a few moments more.

I hear a soft movement and look around.

Gormlaith is on her knees. She presses her head on the deck.

I get up quietly and kneel beside her. I put my hand on the middle of her back and lean close.

"My blood came," she whispers. "My blood came too. Thanks be to our merciful Lord."

As long as her blood flows, no men will pull her away from under our blanket at night. As long as her blood returns every month, there is no child within her. She's crying.

Women must have been the first makers of calendars.

I get up and stand at the side of the ship when Clay Man calls, "Aist?"

I turn around.

Splash. A bucket of frigid water hits me in the chest.

I almost scream. Almost.

I wrap myself in a blanket and lean against a mast.

Clay Man puts his fists on his hips.

I shut my eyes.

I have very little power. But I have no doubt anymore: What power I have comes from my silence.

CHAPTER THIRTEEN:
RIVERS

I wake alone. During the night I rolled out from under the blanket. So did others. It's cool, but definitely not cold any longer.

A city appears ahead. Not just a little gathering of houses. We have passed several little gatherings of houses. This is a real city. A pulse comes alive in my neck. For the first time since Brigid left, hope stirs: A big city means a chance for escape. And the odds are favorable: thirteen to eight.

I walk to Maeve. Gormlaith comes up on my other side. The ship anchors.

We eat.

Clay Man shouts orders. Club Fist and Leering Man tie all our hands behind our backs. The man is not as stupid as I wish he was. We will not escape here.

Clay Man leaves. All seven of the rest of the crew stay behind. I don't understand. It doesn't take seven to guard us, especially with our hands tied.

In late morning Scar Face gives a cry. We look to our

rear. Another boat approaches, hugging the shoreline. It's much smaller than ours. Immediately the crew members rush around gagging us, while Wolf Hound and Scar Face keep us silent with the threat of their spears. We are herded together to the center of the deck and forced to sit. They spread blankets over us, covering our heads. We are a mountain of secret cargo.

Calls come, muffled by our blankets. Someone from our ship exchanges greetings with someone in the smaller boat. It must be alongside us now.

I hear a scream. It sounds distant. People run across the deck. There's the sound of splashing. Soon there are thumps on the deck. Three of them. And the sound of people climbing back on the ship.

When they finally take the blankets off us, we don't see the smaller boat. But there are more prisoners. Two women and a child. They are gagged. Their hands are tied behind their backs. But they aren't blindfolded. Clay Man always blindfolds new prisoners. And there's something else different about these prisoners too. They don't thrash or kick. They look resigned, even the child, who seems to methodically take us all in, one by one, without a blink of horror or even fear.

I walk up beside one of the women. She turns her back on me and looks out to sea.

I glance down at her tied hands. The knot on it is different from the knot our crew use. She was already a prisoner. She's been a prisoner for who knows how long. And she was probably taken from the other side of this sea—from the direction she keeps looking toward.

And that must be why Clay Man left all the crew behind when he went into the city—not to guard us, but so that our ship wouldn't be plundered by another.

Our crew are all here, but not entirely intact. One of the silent men who never interacts with us has a puncture wound on his leg. And Scar Face has a gash across his forehead—parallel to the scar. I wonder how many scars he has under his clothes. Neither of them makes any noise about it.

Out of the corner of my eye, I see the new child prisoner watching me. That child followed my eyes as they assessed the crew. The knowledge creeps around my ears, making them tingle. I move to the side of the ship and stand alone, wary.

Clay Man returns near dusk with another man who has a very long mustache. They come in a small boat and tie it up alongside ours. This man is dressed well: tall boots, skin trousers and tunic, and a fur hat.

Maybe he is a man of learning. A man of honor. I hold my head higher and try to meet his eyes.

Clay Man gives a surprised glance at the two new women and the new child. He takes in the blood on Wounded Man's leg and the gash on Scar Face's forehead. But he quickly recovers himself and says something to the well-dressed man.

The man looks us over appraisingly. His eyes linger on the children. He and Clay Man talk, getting louder, with gestures that make it clear they're bargaining. This well-dressed man has come to buy slaves.

The man strokes the tips of his mustache. He gives Clay Man a small sack.

Clay Man tosses the sack in his hand and looks satisfied. He says something to the Slav children. They go to the well-dressed man, who lifts each one over the side into his boat. And they're gone. Sold. A huge sense of loss flattens me.

But I cannot just stand here, staring after them. Everyone's sitting now. It's mealtime. We eat bread. City bread. Clay Man has brought other city food too—a stew that boasts the aroma of strange spices. But only the crew get it, not the prisoners. Is this because it's a limited treat? Or is it because he's going to sell all the rest of us off now too, so the fattening-up period is over?

I walk to the large cooking pot and look within. There's plenty for everyone. I ladle some into a bowl and hand it to Maeve, who passes it to a child. I fill another bowl and another and another, until Maeve has served us all.

As I lift a spoon to my mouth, I also lift my chin and eyes to Clay Man. He blinks, then shakes his head ruefully.

Everyone talks now. Even the two new women and the new child. They speak among themselves in yet another language—not Gaelic, not William's, not Markus's, and not Russian. But this other language feels familiar. I am almost sure it is Norse. I am on this ship because of an offense a criminal Norseman gave my brother—because my father needed to avenge that offense.

But at least the odds are improving. We are only twelve to the crew's eight, but more of us are adults now.

After the meal, we are gagged and our hands are tied behind our backs again. We pull up anchor and sail. Soon the men take up the oars as well. We turn up a river. Progress is slow because we're going against the current. But the wind is with us. The water ruffles. We travel the rest of the day on this narrow river.

Dark comes late. It's balmy tonight. We anchor in a small, swampy inlet. This is only the second river we have been on, and this one couldn't be more different from that first one.

My eyes glaze over with unshed tears. Inside my head,

I am back on the first river. The night was cold. She had only her tunic. My sister, my little friend. I know now that we were in the land of the *Dubhgall*—the darker Vikings. Maeve told me. So the people along that river speak Norse. Brigid knew no Norse.

The youth from Saxon Britain might have stayed with her. He was a quick thinker, a quick doer. He proved that when he jumped over the side of the ship. And I know there was a core of decency in him, for he and William had tried to fight the crew when they first assaulted Gormlaith. He would have known that Brigid needed his help. But he was even more inadequately dressed than she was. And how would a British peasant come to speak any Norse?

Even if they stayed together, they were lost children in a hostile land.

I should have held Brigid's hand, held on to her tight, kept her with me, sides touching. *Immalle*, like Mother said. I should have clutched her to me—that's what I should have done.

A long brown lock hangs down my breast. It curls just like Brigid's. I look down at myself. I'm taller than her, of course; and bigger all over. But we're both thin, really—as alike as two bean pods, just in different sizes.

She's smarter than me, though. I counted on that intelligence far too much—it was unfair of me to depend on it like that. She's only eight. An eight-year-old has poor judgment. An eight-year-old jumps into a freezing river. I should have clutched her to me.

I pray for her safety.

And for my own.

I turn and see Morc peeking out from the pile of Irish children sleeping near the forward mast. He seems pleased when our eyes meet. He rolls onto his side and his eyelids drift shut.

I can do more than pray. And I have. I failed to help Brigid back then, but I am not failing to help the others now. It's because of me they got blankets in the frigid weather. It's because of me they got stew tonight. I don't know the limits of what Clay Man will allow, but I will protect all of us as best I can.

◆ ◆ ◆

This morning we land on a lakeside. Last night we passed a town without stopping; Clay Man clearly wanted to push us on to enter this large green lake before nightfall. Our hands are free as we climb over the side of the ship, but the crew have gagged us again. This is my first time on land since I was captured. The mucky ground comes at me too firm and too still. I stumble on stumpy feet.

Everyone else stumbles around me. I'd like to lie down and roll. Just roll and roll and roll, feeling the earth immobile under me.

The crew take barrels and chests out of the ship and put them on the ground. But they leave the oars and ropes and blankets on board.

All help but Wounded Man. He limps. Every step brings a wince. The hole in his leg must be festering.

The crew pull the shallow ship onto the swampy grasses and lift it. Clay Man carries a whip. He says something to William and points to a spot on the side of the ship. William runs to that spot and helps lift the ship.

Maeve and Gormlaith and the two Norse women and I help carry that ship too. The Norse child and Markus carry a chest between them. The four Irish children manage a chest among them. Leering Man stays behind with the extra cargo. Clay Man leads the way. Wounded Man hobbles behind.

We portage the ship and those chests through the grasses and over a little hillock to another river. Then we put it into the water. Scar Face and Club Fist lift us prisoners into the ship. They lift in Wounded Man, too. He flinches when they touch him.

Scar Face and Club Fist stand guard over us while the rest of the crew goes back and forth with William and Markus until all the cargo is here. They load it and we're off again.

The whole thing takes most of the day. It's exhausting. And Leering Man got bitten by some sort of insect. His arm is swollen and red.

Mustache Man is lucky enough to take down a buck with an arrow. He skins it in the middle of the deck. When he finishes, I push him aside with a warning glance at Clay Man. Then Maeve and Gormlaith and I prepare the meat.

"We could poison them," says Gormlaith almost casually. Maeve doesn't answer; her face barely changes. But it's the truth; this is the first time we've been the ones to cook. I watch Gormlaith's every move breathlessly. If she produces a vial of toxins from the folds of her shift, what will I do? Killing is a mortal sin.

Gormlaith simply stirs the meat in the pot and gazes off somewhere. And I realize poison is but her dream. She has so much to hate them for.

"Here." Maeve fishes the liver and the heart from the bubbling stew and drops them into a bowl. "These are for the children. They're next, of course." I stare at her. Next for what? For being sold? "You give it to them, Aist."

Me, the captive, I am to walk past the captors with something they want in my hands. I rise to the challenge and accept the bowl as though it's sacred. The crew lift their noses to the wonderful smell as I carry it across the deck. I grow almost giddy with audacity. But Clay Man doesn't even blanch when I set the bowl down in the center of the circle of children. Maybe Maeve's right and he knows they need it most. Or maybe he merely senses I'd fight him hard.

We all eat well.

The crew sing after dinner. They join us around Maeve when she tells stories. I've seen them listening before. But this is the first time they've actually come to sit among us.

Clay Man sits beside me.

I pull my knees up to my chest and wrap my arms around them. This way I feel impenetrable.

The wind never stops.

◆　◆　◆

Two days later we portage again. It's a shorter distance this time. We are now on the third river. And the current of this one is different. We're still going south, but now we're going with the current, so even though the flow is slow and gentle, we're moving faster. This river is wider, too, with more settlements along it. But we don't stop.

The right bank is still rolling hills with groves of trees and quiet lakes that give themselves away by how they reflect the sunlight. Any native of Eire can spot a lake from far, even small ones. But the left bank is flat land as far as I can see. Just grass and swamp.

Something is different about today. The crew are more alert. And Scar Face said something that made the other crew members laugh. Plus Leering Man's arm is fine now and Wounded Man's leg seems to be hurting him less. In all, they're as close to happy as I've seen them.

I sight the city in late afternoon, and I know immediately that this is what the crew have been looking forward to. It's enormous, spreading out on both sides of the river, with a low, thatched-roof fortress near the water.

The crew scurry around, dealing with the details of landing and securing the sails and oars. They push us prisoners together and Mustache Man comes around tying our hands.

"Kiev," says Maeve in my ear.

I don't know what that means. I cock my head at her.

"It's an even bigger city than Smolensk," she says.

How does she know the names of these places? I want to ask her. How do you know what the crew members say? Do you really understand Russian? Who are you, Maeve?

"You give yourself away in too many ways," says Maeve. "I know who you are."

My mouth now drops fully open.

Maeve shakes her head. "No, no, of course I don't know your name. To me you are only dear Aist. But I know you are royalty. The way you turned under Gormlaith's and my hands as we washed you—that told me you were used to being served. And, of course, I knew it from the ring that now hangs from the captain's neck. Don't give anything else away, Aist."

Her speech ends as she is gagged. Everyone is gagged.

The crew wash their faces. Clean shirts come out of the chests. They smooth their hair in place with river water. And they go ashore. Only Clay Man and Club Fist stay behind to guard us.

The day drags into evening. I stand by the rail and look out at the water. A wind rises and whips my hair across my eyes and I'm reminded of the night I climbed to the top of the fort wall in Downpatrick, the night before Brigid and I left home. A shiver shoots up my spine. The Norse child comes to stand beside me. The child is as tall as me, though very thin, and as I look at those fine cheekbones I realize with surprise that this is a girl, probably just about my age. She turns, and her eyes take me in kindly. Lord, how I wish she was Brigid.

165

✦ ✦ ✦

The water is growing white and frothy. I can hear cascades beyond.

Our ship goes to shore and we prepare to portage.

The Norse girl comes up beside me, a habit she's formed lately, but what's new is that she chatters happily. She's talked to me a few times since that day in Kiev. But never so vigorously. And never in a way I could understand. This time, though, I know she's talking about the white water. She circles my waist with her arm and draws me to her side and keeps chattering and pointing with the other hand. I don't pull away.

Once all the cargo is out on shore, we take our usual positions, and Leering Man stays behind with the extra cargo like usual.

But there are two differences. Wounded Man isn't with us. He never returned to the ship after his night in Kiev. So now the crew number only seven.

The second difference is that Scar Face and Club Fist don't help carry the ship. Instead they stand ready with spears. They run back and forth beside the ship as we carry it. They look in all directions.

Clay Man leads the way, and he's carrying a spear too. They're afraid of attack. But who would be out here to attack us? There's no town nearby. Could there be raiding nomads?

We move faster than normal, even though we are short two people on carrying the ship's weight. Fear speeds us.

I'm lucky I'm on the side of the ship near the river so I can see it as we walk. There are no waterfalls, but there are raging rapids.

The Norse girl is on the far side of the ship. I wish she was over here. I wish I could tell her what I'm seeing.

We ride in the ship again, only to have to get out and portage once more. Then another time. And another.

In all, we pass seven sets of rapids. And the Norse girl and I trade positions deliberately each time, in silent agreement, so that both of us get to see them.

When we're all finally back in the ship for good again, we have a treat of bread and honey. That's something the crew brought back from their night in Kiev. We each get a single piece, but it feels like a feast.

Clay Man watches me eat my last bite. He comes over and gives me a second piece of bread with more honey. There's a curve to his shoulder, a slackness to his cheek. He says something short. Just a word or two. I fear it's an endearment.

The bread sits in my hand heavy as gold. The honey smells so sweet I could swoon.

The prisoners' eyes are immediately on me. I want this bread and honey. I want it. But the cost may be too high.

I take a bite, then I go from prisoner to prisoner, giving each a bite. Lips and teeth, they are reduced to lips and teeth and an occasional tongue. And, oh, yes, eyes that register at once incomprehension and gratitude. We are careful to make it stretch to the very last one.

I don't look at Clay Man. But later, when I hear him talking to someone and I am sure he is not looking at me, I lick the last of the honey from my fingers.

I see the Norse girl glance at me. She gives a quick smile and looks away.

The ship goes rapidly for the rest of the day. The land is forested now, though the trees are mostly low, like in Eire. The river is in a valley, and there are fewer tributaries than before. We pass through one very narrow rocky spot and skirt around a big island of pitch-black soil and then it's just smooth sailing, with almost no turns anymore, all the way to a giant sea.

CHAPTER FOURTEEN: THE SLAVE MARKET

"This city is Miklagard," says Maeve to the Irish children. But, really, all of us are listening to her. Even the ones who don't speak Gaelic. It's habit by now.

When we moored our boat at dawn, Maeve told us that sea inlet forms the most perfect harbor in the world, called the Golden Horn. Ever since then she's been spouting facts, educating us. Three parallel stone and rubble walls surround this enormous city. The outermost one is dotted with giant towers. Maeve says there are one hundred towers in all, and I believe she does not exaggerate, for the wall stretches far beyond the eye's ability to see. The innermost wall is as high as the foothills of Ulster.

"Miklagard is the second largest city in the world, after Särkland," booms Maeve's voice. "It's the capital of Byzans and the center of Christianity."

Byzans? We have gone around to the far side of the world, then. In just three months. My body keeps track of the months all on its own. I turn in a circle and stare.

Everywhere I look there are hills with giant churches topped by enormous domes. Ahead of us is a red cathedral that seems more a fortress than a church.

"And those," says Gormlaith, "are Arabs, right?" She points.

"Exactly," says Maeve. "They're Muslim. It's a religion that isn't Christian and isn't heathen."

We stare at men with white cloth on their heads and flowing tunics that cover their arms and go all the way to the ground. It must be hard living here dressed like that. It's stunningly hot.

I've heard of heat like this. Foreign travelers passing through Eire sometimes talked of deserts. But nothing they said could have prepared me. The sun beats like a slave master. The air shimmers, making colors—red, yellow, green. We've been off the ship only since dawn and already my tongue is so dry, it threatens to turn to dust. Breathing is a chore.

"And what are those?" Morc points to tall brown animals with long curvy necks and humps on their backs.

"Camels," says Maeve. "Arabs ride them like horses."

I look at her with gratitude. Without Maeve, I sometimes think I might go mad. How she came to know so much of the world I cannot guess. If I could talk now, though, I wouldn't ask her. My silence may be the source of my power in an obvious, if inexplicable, way, but all of us draw something from what we do not tell.

Clay Man gives orders, and Wolf Hound and Mustache Man tie us together with ropes around our waists. But our hands are free and our mouths are not gagged. We've been expecting something like this, of course. It's time to sell us.

Clay Man ties my rope to a rope around his waist. We are one long line now with Clay Man at the head.

Maeve is right behind me. "You're his prized possession," she says in my ear. "He's taken a fancy to you."

My mind shuts tight, so that for a brief while I cannot see or hear or smell or feel anything. But then, like hot rain, the thought falls: You knew this. This is not new terrible information. You knew this. Maeve has just confirmed it. That's all.

Clay Man looks at me with concern. I must have paled. I'm me again. Alive. And the last thing I want is Clay Man's concern. I will myself to raise my head.

Clay Man has cleaned himself up for today. His hair is combed. But my three stork feathers still stick up from the top of his head. He pats them now. A leather bag hangs from his waist. It's wet. He holds a second leather bag in his hand. It's dry. Now he tucks the dry bag under one arm and we're off.

We walk in silence, going wherever Clay Man leads us. Wolf Hound and Mustache Man walk on either side. Club Fist walks behind us. The other three—Scar Face, Leering Man, and the remaining silent man who never interacts with us—go off on their own. We take the main road, which, judging by the sun, runs west from the harbor. It's decorated with statues of lions and columns that mark the entrances to fancy shops for copperware and glass and leather goods. I remember how impressed I was with the main streets of Dublin, but those Viking shops were shadows compared to Miklagard's grand stores.

The road opens into a market square now. Vendors hawk plants, birds, clothes, all packed together in a tight, continuous flow of colors. One boy runs up to me holding out a straw box so loosely woven that I can see the small creature inside. Maeve shooes him away and tells us that with one sting, that creature—a scorpion—can kill us. We close ranks.

Clay Man talks to a man who is dressed just like he is. A Russian. The man moves his wares aside to make room for us. Clay Man has us sit on the ground in a circle, with him kneeling, still attached to me by that rope.

He opens his leather bag and takes out a metal contraption and sets it up and attaches measuring pans. It's a scale, cleverly designed. The hinged arms collapse inward, folding into a line with the hanger bar. The measuring pans nest within each other, so that all parts fit neatly in that trim bag.

Now he takes out his weights. They're made of clay. He sets them on the ground beside the scale, but one drops and breaks. I watch as he opens the wet leather bag and takes out a small pot of clay. He has a few long fingernails—the ones I felt dig into me when he first captured me—and he uses them now to shave off small amounts of clay. Quickly he fashions a new weight, holds it on his fingertips, then adds a bit more clay. The speed of work, the sureness of his actions, fascinate me.

Clay Man looks sideways at me and catches me watching him. He lifts an eyebrow and takes a silver coin out of a pouch inside his shirt. He puts the coin in one measuring pan and the new weight in the other pan. The new weight is heavier than the coin.

Now Clay Man takes out his oil lamp and lights it. He holds the new clay weight in metal tongs above the small flame, turning it over and over, till it dries. Then he snuffs out the lamp and puts the new weight back in the pan. It's exactly equal to the silver coin. Exactly. He knew that when it was dry, that clay weight would be the precise weight of that silver coin.

Clay Man grins at me in pride. Then he busies himself putting away his clay.

"A dirham," whispers Maeve. "That's the standard coin from here east and south, across the Arab empires. Everything is sold for dirhams."

Such tiny coins. In Eire we measure prices in heifers, hogs, sheep—whatever we have. But here they use coins. They're shiny and beautiful, yes. But flimsy. They weigh practically nothing—the weight of a pinch of clay. It would take two thousand of them at least to weigh as much as the Irish stone.

Clay Man checks to see if I'm still watching him. When he sees I am, he grins again.

And now I understand his odor—his defining odor. Clay Man smells of the clay he uses for his weights. I wonder if he knows that. I wonder if he realizes he is always a slave dealer. He can never be a confiding friend, a tender father, a passionate lover without that fact intruding. He reeks of his profession. And now I realize that the reason we are tied is not to keep us from escaping—no, no, there's nowhere to escape to in this slave market. We are tied to keep us together so no one can steal any of us.

I knew this was coming. It's all been leading here. I knew it.

An Arab walks up and talks with Clay Man. Wolf

Hound comes forward and helps in the negotiations; why, he speaks Arabic.

The Arab man is small and thin. His face is lined and leathery. And closed. From it I read nothing about the kind of man he is, the kind of master he will be.

A man and woman stand by the side and watch the exchange. They are dressed in tunics, not Arab garb. And their skin and hair reveal them as northerners. Christians. I interlace my fingers and press my hands together hard. Those Christians know better. Their priests must preach it to them, just as the priests in Eire do. They should protest—object that slavery is a blot on mankind. They should not just watch!

The Arab now gives a quick bob of the head and walks past Clay Man. He looks into the Irish children's mouths and into their eyes, which have now become wild. He examines their feet. He pulls up their tunics and checks their bottoms.

I glare at him. Blood pumps in the sides of my neck.

Riley sobs. Kacey lets out a series of little yelps. Morc and Patrick-Nyle squirm and kick frantically. Maeve squeezes my arm so hard, it takes all my efforts not to scream.

Club Fist comes around and sits in front of Maeve, facing her. He is the brute. His very presence is a threat.

Maeve's hand falls away from my arm. I sense her whole body sag.

The Arab pays for the children in silver dirhams and leads them away. The children don't look back.

And it all happened with those good Christians looking on. My stomach turns. I am woozy.

Maeve turns her head away. Gormlaith puts her hands on Maeve's shoulders and pulls her in, folding her arms around her. But Gormlaith doesn't cry. Her eyes rage. The greater surprise is that Maeve now does, for the first time. I never heard any of the children call her mother. But they did other things. They were hers, of course—all but Riley.

The two Norse women and the Norse girl hold on to one another.

Markus and William huddle together.

All of us knew this was coming. But nothing could have prepared us. Maeve even said the children were next—she said those very words when we cooked the venison the night after the Slav children were sold. But even she wasn't prepared. We look at Maeve and our hearts break for her.

Lord, I miss Brigid.

Clay Man goes about his business as though nothing of import has happened. He uses the weights to assure himself again of the proper value of the silver. Some of the coins go safely in a pouch inside his shirt. Others he quickly slips into another pouch hanging from his belt.

He urges us to our feet and we follow him through the market, while he uses those coins to buy things. Wolf Hound and Mustache Man and Club Fist carry everything he buys.

We are like useless beasts. We do not even look at what Clay Man buys. We keep our eyes on the ground and do nothing but let ourselves be herded.

We eat in the market. Strange food that makes my stomach churn. We return to the ship to sleep. I lie in the open and look up at stars.

The Norse girl comes and lies beside me. "*Himni*," she says. "*Fóru lausar undir himni.*"

I don't know what that means. But I know she's talking about the sky.

I close my eyes. I don't sleep.

+ + +

In the morning we file out again. Eight of us. Our eyes shine. We jump at every touch. Inside my head is a continual scream. The day is long and painful. At night we return to the ship, only four left: Gormlaith, Maeve, the Norse girl, and me.

The Norse girl lies beside me on the deck again. And she talks of *himni* once more. And of *máni* and *stjörnur*. She points at the moon and the stars. She cried when the Norse women were sold, but I'm pretty sure that neither was her mother. They looked very little alike. She cries again now.

Gormlaith cried when Markus and William were sold. She couldn't even speak with them, but she cried. Maybe because she felt they deserved it; everyone deserves to be cried for. I cannot hear if she's crying now, though. She's lying on the far side of Maeve, who has said nothing since the children left.

I stare at the heavens, my eyes so dry they burn. Gormlaith, Maeve, the Norse girl, and me. We are next.

I close my eyes. We are all the same now, the four of us. One future. No past.

Sleep comes instantly.

✦ ✦ ✦

Someone jerks me awake, pulling on my elbow. I sit up. It's Clay Man. He pulls me over to his lit lamp. On the deck he has spread out coins. He shows them to me, talking in a gruff whisper.

I don't care to look. What does it matter?

Clay Man shakes his head. He goes over and wakes up Maeve. She stumbles to the lamp with him. Clay Man talks again. Then he pokes Maeve. And she talks.

She explains the coins to me. On one side are numbers: the year the coins were struck according to the Islamic calendar. On the other side are the places they were struck: Baghdad, Cairo, Damascus, Isfahan, Tashkent. Some coins have words—quotations from the Koran, the Islamic holy book.

Clay Man is animated. His hands fly. He pokes Maeve hard. She talks more. I don't really think she's translating, though. I don't think she speaks his language. She just knows what the coins are all about. Maybe she tells me more than Clay Man even says. She's smarter than him.

Finally she says to me, "Humor him or we will never sleep. Act impressed at how much he knows. Smile."

I widen my eyes at Clay Man.

It's enough. He puts out the lamp. We all sleep.

✦   ✦   ✦

In the morning we assume our usual post in the market. A Russian man comes up and points to the stork feathers in Clay Man's hair and talks excitedly. Clay Man steps back, touching the feathers protectively. The man holds out a coin. Money for stork feathers? Clay Man looks at me and says, *"Aist."* The Russian man stares at me. Clay Man adds, *"Charodeitsa."*

The Russian man immediately averts his eyes. *"Charodeitsa,"* he repeats in a hushed voice. He hurries away.

Maeve looks at me and raises an eyebrow. Does she know what that word means?

A fat Arab approaches gingerly. He touches Gormlaith on the shoulder. She shrinks away. He draws back timidly. He touches Maeve. She jerks her head around and glares at him. The Norse girl and I move together. But the fat Arab doesn't look at us. He's intent on Gormlaith. His mouth hangs opens, he's so excited. He negotiates with Clay Man. Coins change hands. He leads Gormlaith away. My cheeks are so heavy, I think they will fall away from my skull.

Maeve's arms circle me from behind. She rests on my back and whispers in my ear. "He can't be any worse than what she's had so far."

Clay Man passes the rest of the day trading coins for reams of silk, boxes of pearls, satchels of spices. We eat and return to the ship.

In the night someone rolls against me as we lie sleeping. I open my eyes to see Maeve's eyes shining at me in the moonlight. "He's convinced you are an *aist*—a stork," she whispers. "A stork who has the power to change form into a woman. He thinks you may be a *charodeitsa*—an enchantress, but unlike our Irish *piseogaí*, he fears you could be evil. It's only how clean and pretty you are that keeps him from quaking."

I'm stunned, both because it's clear she does know Russian, or at least some words of it, and because of what she has said.

"Once I am gone . . ."

I open my mouth to protest and wish just this once that I could speak.

". . . once I am gone, you must continue the ruse. You must never speak."

I gulp down the searing fluid that has risen from my stomach and force myself to hold together and pay attention. This sounds like Gospel. I wait for more guidance, but Maeve seems to have lost energy. I reach for her hand and pull.

"He won't sell you. And he dares not mistreat you." Her voice catches. "Good-bye, dear Aist." She rolls away again.

So many things make sense now. How he tried over and over to get me to speak. He tested me. And I passed, because of Maeve and a vow to Brigid to stay silent. Silent as a stork.

I want to sweep Maeve's words away in helpless anger,

but they won't go. I get drunk on them. I am far from helpless, actually. I have as much power as if I really were an enchantress.

Maybe that's how magic works. Maybe all you need is for someone to believe in you.

+ + +

Morning comes. We go to the market. And it happens as she said: Clay Man sells Maeve. It takes all I have not to collapse.

The Norse girl drapes her arms over me lightly, as though mimicking the way Maeve behaved the day before. She blows cooling air on my temples. She murmurs in my ear. She says words I heard the Norse women say to her. And I know she's telling me that I can make it through this. Without understanding the words, I understand the message.

I know the message is true. I wish it wasn't. I wish I could just turn into vapor. Disappear.

The day passes.

The Norse girl holds up her hands and says a word. She points at her shoes and says a word. She touches her nose and says a word. Then she says the first word again and waits.

It takes a second before I understand. I point at her hands. She tells me how smart I am. Then she says another word. I point at her nose. She cheers and kisses my cheek.

She names the objects around us. Tunic, eyes, teeth, arms, hair. She teaches me her name—Thora—and she calls me Aist. I listen and learn. What else is there to do?

In the middle of our lessons, an old man comes to inspect Thora and me. It becomes clear that Clay Man's going to sell Thora, but not me.

Clay Man takes coins and goes to untie Thora's rope from mine.

Thora. She's all I have left.

I step in the way. I lift my chin straight up to the sky and open my mouth wide in a silent scream. Then I look through him, as though I have the power to wither him to nothing.

Clay Man's hands go to his chest. He walks a few steps backward. He gives the old man back the coins.

Clay Man ties me to him again, waist to waist, and we walk the market in a line: Clay Man, me, Thora. Defiance starts in my toes and rises to my ankles. It makes me walk slowly. So slowly, Clay Man has to match his pace to mine, or else face dragging me stumbling along. He says something to me—words I know mean to hurry. But I don't.

And he slows down. I knew he would. Thora keeps

her eyes on the ground through all this. I have no idea what she thinks.

Clay Man buys buttons, arm rings, neck rings. All of silver. He buys carnelian and rock crystal beads. He buys sword chapes with the shapes of falcons and hawks on them. He shows me everything. But defiance has now risen all the way to my eyes. I look away. I am not a magic being. But I am my parents' daughter. I am Brigid's sister. I am a princess. I walk tall like a stork.

I belong to no one. Like a stork.

Thora's eyes go from Clay Man to me and back. Then she stares at the ground again.

Clay Man gives up on trying to impress me with jewels. He buys me strange food. He's not stupid; he knows how hungry I've been. It dawns on me that he's been hungry before. Savagely so. He understands the need. Underneath everything, he understands.

We eat.

CHAPTER FIFTEEN:
PRÆLAR

Thora and I walk the hills outside the town of Hyllestad, up in the southwestern part of the north country. We're collecting wild herbs and legumes to dry and put into boxes—a typical morning chore. The rest of the slave girls who live with us aren't far off. We can see them in the distance picking plants, just like us. It's a rule that we all have to stay within sight of one another.

Thora nudges me.

I look where she's pointing.

Two *prælar*—slaves—are carrying a small wooden chest, following their master off into the hills. The master carries two shovels.

"That chest holds the master's silver hoard," says Thora. "Jewelry, buckles, coins. They're going to bury it someplace secret in case there's a retaliatory attack from the south. Remember them," she says. "Later, when they return, watch what happens. You'll see I'm right."

Thora speaks Norse to me. And I understand her. Not always entirely, but most of the time well enough.

We've been together for only a few months. But she's my constant companion, and she chatters nonstop.

"Here, eat this." Thora rips me a long blade of grass and sticks one into her own mouth.

I chew on it and shiver from the sour taste.

"Isn't it great?" Suddenly she furrows her brow. "Don't chew grasses at random, though. Some can be poisonous. You know what that means, right?" She narrows her eyes at me, as though she's trying to figure out if I'm a half-wit or not. "Listen, just eat what I eat, and you'll be all right." Thora knows all these plants, for this is her homeland. Not this very town, but somewhere north of here. Thora's been all over this land in her short life.

The *þræll* girls we live with now come from the north shores along the East Sea. Clay Man either stole them or bought them for practically nothing on his way across from Russia. As each one joined us, Thora greeted her and asked all about her. I listened, but my Norse wasn't so good then, not nearly as good as it is now, and I didn't catch details. Some of them have been bought and sold over and over. Thora has. She's been a *þræll* since she was six, in three different countries already. And she pays attention. By this point, she knows a lot about the world.

I wonder if Maeve had been a *þræll* before.

Up ahead I see a tall stone cross. I stop and look from it to Thora.

"It's a quarry," says Thora. She's gotten very good at answering my eyes. "Hyllestad is famous for its stone. And there are lots of carvers here. That cross has been set near the road, ready to be fetched by the buyer."

I'm confused. A cross? This town isn't Christian, I know that very well. It's heathen, like most Norse towns. In fact, last week a boatload of townsmen set off south toward a Norse settlement to burn a church. That's why people here are preparing in case of retaliation; that's why that man and his *þrælar* went off to bury his treasures.

I've eavesdropped as men from the town explained all this to Clay Man. They said Christianity is creeping up through the countryside like a disease, threatening their gods: Odin and his son Thor, and Vanir, who is really a group of gods in one—including the fertility god and goddess, Frey and Freya. There are other gods too. Lots of them. So many I can't keep them straight, no matter how many times Thora tells me about them. The heathen church-burners are warriors for their religion, the poor fools. They don't know anything about salvation. I heard a man say they are determined to stomp out Christianity before it reaches the Viking stronghold at the mouth of the River Nidelva, to the north.

Those words made my throat close. The River Nidelva is where Bjarni came from, the Viking who wanted to marry me. The Viking who either is now at the bottom of the harbor in Downpatrick or who killed my family.

I face Thora and put my hands on her shoulders and furrow my forehead and raise my brows. I need for her to understand, to answer me: What are these heathens doing, making stone crosses?

She tilts her head. "Want to go see it? Don't worry. A Christian cross can't hurt you. Come on." She walks off.

I'm beside her in an instant. And I realize I can answer my own question: These people are practical. I've been watching them interact with Clay Man long enough to know that. Their dislike for him shows in their faces, but they trade with him anyway. So why should they hesitate to fill an order for a cross that will sit in a church or in a Christian graveyard? Business is business, after all. I remember the Christians in Miklagard who watched the slave trade in their own market and didn't say a word. Heathens or Christians, it doesn't matter—business is business.

Thora and I walk solemnly toward the stone cross. The closer we get, the more I realize that it's unusually large. It towers above us. It might be double our height. I walk around to the front, look up, and both hands fly to my mouth, I'm so startled.

"What is it?" Thora smoothes my hair. It's such a natural act, but so unexpected that I cling to her. "What happened?" she says tenderly. I lead Thora with my eyes to the image.

Carved into the stone right where the two parts of the cross come together is an animal, a darling four-footed animal. I recognize it. It's the same creature I saw on the silver brooch in Dublin. But while the silver brooch was deceptively delicate in its charm, here the things that curl around the animal are not vines, but vipers. They circle, ready for the kill. Their fascination is deviant, and fatal. Nothing can save the animal now.

I couldn't save Brigid.

"Is it the runes that frighten you?" Thora stands and touches the linear letters beneath the figure. "Some people think letters are wicked magic. But they're ignorant. I saw an ordinary boy learn to read and write them. He said the runes on stone tablets usually just tell the tales we all know from sitting around the campfire at night. Don't be afraid." She pulls me to my feet. "There's enough real stuff to be afraid of without letting stupidities terrorize us. Come on. We'd better hurry. Gilli's waiting."

Clay Man's name to everyone else is Gilli. And Thora's right; he has stopped out on the road with the rest of his *þrælar*. He's looking back at us with annoyance.

I turn sideways and lift my chin, offering Clay Man my profile. I am as haughty as a princess-made-slave can be— a thought that makes me almost laugh in its pitifulness.

"Don't act stupid, Aist. One of these days, Gilli is going to whip you for not jumping at his orders. Get up."

I count inside my head. It's important to keep Clay Man waiting long enough for him to remember his fears.

"I don't understand why he doesn't beat you, but he'll beat me. I'm going." Thora runs ahead. "Your next owner won't be so daft," she calls back. "He'll whip you blind. Or worse. You'd better learn fast what it means to be a *þræll*. Come on. Please."

Clay Man will never sell me. But Thora's right; he might beat her. I get up and rush after her to catch up with the others.

Still, Thora takes the time to rip out a snatch of grass. She rubs the roots between her hands, holds them to her nose, then to mine. I know this smell; it's vetiver, the aromatic oil Mother puts on her wrists. Her wrists, arms, neck. Her voice. She exists somewhere. Or I hope she does. *Máthir*—Mother. Oh, Lord, what I would give just to see my mother.

Thora takes me by the hand and pulls me. Somehow she knows that's exactly what I need now. Friendship is a blessing.

We walk along the plank road. Pigs cavort in the side ditches. I pinch my nose closed to keep out the stench.

A woman coming from the other direction runs up to me and knocks my hand away from my nose. "Filthy *þræll*. Don't act like that smell bothers you. You ugly thing. Can't even keep your shoes tied."

I look down, curl my shoulders, and walk faster. I am no filthier than she is. And my shoes are tied perfectly.

"Ugly," says Thora in a quiet, low voice, "stupid, clumsy, fool, coward, thief." She says the words in a dull singsong. "Get used to it. Like I told you. They'll say anything, it doesn't matter if it's true or not. You'll see I'm right. Tonight, when that man with the treasure box and the two *þrælar* returns home—you'll see then. Ugly, stupid, clumsy, fool, coward, thief. Everyone hates *þrælar*. You'll see."

Hating *þrælar* makes no sense. People work hard here. We've been here a couple of weeks and Thora explains everything. But I've been watching too, so I know this for myself. Hands are red and rough. Arms and legs are strong as tree trunks from all the physical labor of just plain old daily living. And *þrælar* help at everything. They do the worst jobs. It makes no sense to hate them—to hate us.

We pass the central longhouse, with its high doorsill

191

that Thora told me keeps out the winter snow, and the curving walls and roof, where men attach fresh shingles that reek of pine resin. In the time we've been here, I've never entered the longhouse. Town meetings take place there. And banquets. I wish the muscovite in the window frames allowed a better view inside. Thora says the banquets are a spectacle, with sagas, songs, dancing to harp and pipes. It sounds almost like an Irish celebration.

A man repairs the sides of a boathouse, working cow droppings into the holes between the logs left after the spring thaw. A boy with dark hair, a *þræll* obviously—since most free northerners here have blond hair and blue eyes—sits on the ground nearby. He repairs a net.

Thora follows my eyes. "That's a linen net. For catching salmon and trout in the streams. They get salted or smoked for winter. You can't fish when the streams freeze." Salmon. I love good Irish salmon.

It seems the entire town is remaking itself. Good weather means the workload increases.

The next building we pass is a mystery to me—a Norse home. Every home has thin skin over the windows, like our manor house back in Downpatrick. All I can see from the outside is shadows. And they're mostly up on high stilts anyway. I'd have to go up the ladders to get a really good look—and no one would let me do that.

This one isn't on stilts, though. A woman opens the door and calls to a child playing with a goat.

I lag behind to look through the open door. There's only one room. Tapestries cover the walls, straw covers the floor. The ceiling is painted in rose patterns. Beds are built into the two corners I can see, and there's a long table with two benches down each side and a butter churn on the floor nearby. Chickens peck here and there. A raised fireplace sits right in the center with a smoke hole above it. An iron pot hangs from a rafter over the fire and gives off the sweetest aroma.

I breathe deep and linger. Real families still exist in the world.

"Get on with you, nasty thing!" shouts the woman.

Her tone breaks the spell. My eyes dart to her face, but any trace of motherliness that might usually be there has been masked by her hatred of *prælar*. I hurry to catch up with Thora.

"That's cowberries with honey and pears boiled together," she says, knowing immediately why I lingered. "It's one of the best smells ever."

It's a good smell, but there are much better ones. I remember Brigid and me trying to stave off hunger our second day away from home. We stood by the stork mustering and I talked of bread dipped in hot sheep milk.

Brigid talked of cakes fried in pig fat. Both smell better than this cowberry mess. I blink back tears.

I bet everyone in town knows what that family's eating today. They can't help but know. The houses cluster with small gardens between—herbs, leeks, beans, peas. Outside town lie fields of barley for beer, rye for bread, flax for cloth. On hills overlooking the bay livestock graze. But all is close. No one's ever out of shouting distance, of course. In Eire a person can survive alone. They can't here, not if the winters are as savage as Thora says.

We catch up with the rest of the slave girls and devote the rest of the day to our assigned chores near the tent Clay Man has erected for us. It's pitched on the gravelly shore within sight of the boat; Clay Man trusts no one.

I do these chores carefully. Clay Man orders me, of course, just as he orders the others. But we both know that if I were to stop, he wouldn't do anything about it. I do them of my own free will, because they help me.

We walk up the shore past the last home of this town to where black and gray rocks jut out into the sea. Many are white washed with the excrement of seagulls. The spots capped with tufts of grass and weeds are above the high-water mark, and that's where the gulls make their nests. As seagulls swirl overhead, we collect the warm eggs, dark green with black speckles. The nests hold one or two or even three eggs. And now and then there's an egg just lying out on the bare rock, in the middle of dried-out barnacles and crushed shells. In the scoop of my tunic I hold twenty eggs and carry them all back to our tent without cracking any.

We walk out to the farms where people raise cattle and sheep and goats. The farmers catch the animals and tie them up for us, but we have to do the rest. We break into pairs. Thora and I are a team, of course. I hold the animal's head as still as I can while she milks it. It's hard, milking. Thora tried to teach me on a goat, because she says goats are the easiest. You put four fingers around a teat and close the thumb on the front. Then you press from the index finger down, each finger squeezing in turn, and rotating as you go down. I wasn't good at it. But I carry milk buckets on a yoke across my neck and shoulders, filled to the brim, all the way back to our tent without spilling a drop.

Precision is a goal that takes attention. I lose myself in precision—that's the gift of chores, the gift I need.

Industry becomes a friend too. I work swiftly. We gather shellfish for fish bait. We grind rye into flour. We boil herring and seal blubber for lamp oil.

Clay Man lets us save some of the herring, though. It's important to him that we stay healthy, and, according to Thora, nothing brings a heartier look to the face than herring. We eat it with dill. And a soup of nettle, goat milk, pepper, and seagull eggs, all swimming in a wooden bowl.

The girls talk, and I listen to their quick, lively voices. One got pecked by a seagull protecting her eggs. Now everyone talks about when they got harassed by goats, cattle, hogs, chickens. Commiseration binds them.

Late in the afternoon Thora and I are doing the laundry in a big bucket set outside the tent when she hisses, "See?"

I look up.

A man comes down the road we walked earlier as we came in from the hills. I can't see his face at this distance. But I see the shovels in each hand. The man from this morning. He's alone now. He turns onto a side street.

"Come with me. Hurry. We have to get there and back here before Gilli looks for us." Thora grabs me by the hand and we run up the road in the direction the man came from.

It takes only moments to find them. Two *þrælar*, in the ditch. Their throats have been cut. A rat already races greedily up and down the torso of one. I stare till my eyes burn. I shake my head stupidly. How did Thora know they'd be here?

"That's how he keeps the secret of where he buried

his treasure. Only those *þrælar* knew. Now no one does." Thora squeezes my arm till it hurts. "He won't get in trouble, either. Because we're worth nothing."

I shut my eyes against her words. These men were alive not long ago. I see them in my head. I am in the ditch with them. The rat runs on me. Small, scrabbling feet.

We are all the same—every slave is the same. I am those bodies. I am dead.

Thora takes my hands in hers. "Do what Gilli tells you. Don't wind up in a ditch. Don't leave me."

I can't open my eyes. Thora pulls me.

We return and finish the laundry and do other things. I do whatever Thora does without thought until the day finally ends and I lie on the tent floor beside Thora and will myself to sleep.

Someone walks across the floor. It's Leering Man. I can tell from his gait. He grabs one of the *þrælar*.

I knew this would happen sooner or later. These *þrælar* are all girls. Young. And pretty. And even though the crew is all new now except for Leering Man and Club Fist and Clay Man, I expected assaults long ago.

The girl screams.

Clay Man jumps up and shouts at Leering Man. They argue in Russian, but I catch a few words—important ones. They are fighting about money.

Leering Man lets the girl go. He goes out through the tent flaps, leaving one up. Lord help the women of Hyllestad tonight.

And Lord help these new *prælar*. Clay Man is protecting them for a reason. He gathered these particular *prælar*—young and pretty and female—for a purpose. And that purpose can't be good.

When I am sure everyone else is asleep, I sit up. Something glints in the light that seems always to be with us. Clay Man has left a knife with the cooking utensils. A large one, far too heavy and long to hide within my clothing. I pick it up and cut a thin line in my forearm. Blood runs out immediately.

I must still be alive. But the vipers circle.

Thora is right: They hate us. These people hate *prælar*, whether foreigners, like me, or their own stock, like Thora.

I grit my teeth. I wish I were my father. I would free every slave in the kingdom of Downpatrick.

CHAPTER SIXTEEN:
PRICES

Clay Man drops the comb in my lap. "Your turn," he says in Norse.

The other eleven of his young, pretty *þrælar* have already used it willingly. I've hung back. I ceased combing my hair and cleaning my face and washing my clothes back in Hyllestad, when Clay Man stopped Leering Man from assaulting one of us.

Young and pretty. These are key facts. I can't do anything about being young. But I can make myself as far from pretty as possible. I will not be part of Clay Man's plan for us, whatever it is.

I look at Clay Man and toss my clumpy hair defiantly.

His jaw bone moves from side to side. His eyes register fear. That's the effect my filth has on him. I should have done this earlier. Maeve said it was only my cleanliness that kept Clay Man from quaking. Russians believe the worst kind of witches are filthy. Well, now I look like his most beastly nightmare.

I wish Thora would follow my lead. Whenever

she cleans herself, I pull away the rag. She mustn't be pretty—she mustn't be part of Clay Man's scheme. But she simply yanks the rag back.

I stare at Clay Man now, the vision of the evil enchantress he believes I am. Slovenly to the point of despising myself. I will stay like this until I understand what his plan is.

He gives a *humph*. "Come on, everyone, let's go."

We leave the tent Clay Man set up for us last night and follow him, tied together by ropes at the waist, like in the slave market in Miklagard, back in Byzans. But this place is very different.

We are on Brännö Island, still in the land of the Norsemen. Ironically, these criminal northerners have multiple laws. One is that every third summer the local chieftains from all the Norse-speaking countries must make an excursion here. They report in and pay their respects to the king. They discuss legal issues and pass judgments in difficult cases. Sometimes they elect a new king. It's the most important meeting of all.

For the last few nights Clay Man has talked about all the chieftains he expects to see here. He made a fist of one hand and rubbed the other around it as he talked. The list seemed almost a chant. The crew members listened attentively.

They've gone off now, though. They left us last night after helping set up the tent. It's just us and Clay Man this morning.

I look around, fearful at first, but quickly find that nothing seems terribly strange. This is an ordinary Norse settlement, rather small, in fact, though clearly richer than most. Some of the farmhouses have two stories, with huge chimneys. Several are made of stone. Herds of reindeer mingle in pens with goats and cows. But every third summer, when so many people come for these meetings, this little town explodes in size, because the extensive meadow at the edge of town turns into a giant marketplace ringed by tents the visitors have pitched.

There's a festive feeling to everything out in this temporary marketplace. Honey-sweet smells come from a giant makeshift bake house the townsfolk have set up. The aroma of roast boar seeps out of huge eating tents. These summer meetings must play a big role in the island's prosperity.

The townsfolk are not the only ones doing good business, though. Men play harps and lutes in little spots scattered all through the marketplace, while women dance—and passersby stop to watch and throw coins in a bowl. Visiting gamblers thrive, speaking Norse and Russian and other languages I can't identify. Men sit at gaming tables and play chess with pieces made from horse teeth, or backgammon with pieces made from sea green or purple glass. And there's one game I've never seen before that uses red pieces on a square board. The men have one finger hooked through a jug of mead—bog myrtle or hop honey. Strong brew; they grow more boisterous as the morning progresses.

Visiting traders are doing well too. We pass a group of blond and redheaded children with tired eyes, sitting behind a corpulent beast of a man wearing a mustache that drips down to his chest and the unmistakable Russian hat. A slave trader. I know those children are Irish. While he and Clay Man exchange quick greetings in their tongue, I search the faces of the children. No Brigid.

Not all the Russians here are slave traders, though. We walk by some with boxes full of belts. Garnets stud their bronze buckles in hearts or spiral designs. The horse harnesses are gilded. Other traders have sacks of aromatic spices. Money passes hands freely. Lots of it.

One Russian calls out in accented Norse, "Come see. Let your eyes do more than you ever imagined. I just traveled from way down on the Caspian Sea, up along the Volga River, all the way here." He sweeps his arm across the sky as he speaks. "Cut crystals from the Persian town of Basra—that's what I offer you. Splendidly useful. A man can look through them and everything he sees will be magnified many times." He laughs. "You there." He points to a well-dressed man who has stopped to listen. "Look through one of my crystals, and you can discern whether the gems you want to buy are truly flawless or not."

The man shakes his head and moves on.

The vendor clears his throat and turns to another man. He calls, "Come see. Let your eyes do more than you ever imagined. . . ."

But most of the traders we pass have only silk and pots and jewelry and coins—all from Asia. Why can't I find someone with Irish goods? With wool and linen and spinning wheels and weaving looms. Or even with loot from the Irish monasteries. All I need is one trader who will head back to Eire after this meeting. One trader I can somehow get to take me along.

But no luck. Asia, Asia, Asia. Everything is made of Asian silver. Clay Man has a stash of Asian silver goods to trade too. He told me this northern land has no indigenous source of silver, and Vikings are hungry for what is hard to come by. So the Russians bring it to them, at a high price. The Vikings trade them iron, timber, walrus tusks, sable and fox and beaver furs, honey, amber, tar, sealskins, soapstone pots with flat stone covers—all useful things, in exchange for shiny Asian silver.

None of it makes sense to me. And I will always hate silver. All I care about is finding a trader in Irish goods.

"Look," whispers Thora in my ear. She points, using just her eyes, at a passing man. "His shoes. See the high tops? They're made of elk leather. He's from Nidaros, way up north."

Nidaros. Bjarni is from Nidaros.

"Watch the shoes," says Thora. "Each village has its own style. Some from even farther north are made of bear hide. With antler tines."

I think of Irish sweaters—of knit patterns that identify villages, so the lost can be brought back where they belong. I clench my teeth. I'm going home, no matter what. I stare at the ground.

We walk along and Thora whispers now and then. "Deer. Elk. Cow. Moose." And at one point she notes, "Polar bear fangs."

That catches my attention. I look up. The fangs hang as an amulet around a man's neck. We have bears in Eire, of course, but not the big white monsters that Thora has told me about here. Now I want to see polar bear shoes, too.

A man passes leading a reindeer by a rope. The reindeer pulls a sled with a girl sitting on it atop a pile of animal furs. She's young and pretty. He calls out in Norse, "Virgin. Who wants a comely virgin?"

"How much?" asks Clay Man.

"One mark of silver."

That's double what regular slaves go for. I've seen slave trading in every Norse town we've traveled through, and never has a slave, virgin or no, fetched that much.

Clay Man smiles and leads us back to our tent. He had no intention of buying the girl.

And all of a sudden I know Clay Man's plan. Young and pretty. And all of us are virgins. Vikings may despise *þrælar* and call us all sorts of names, but they obviously pay extra for virgins, especially pretty ones. Clay Man has come as a trader, in virgins.

It makes sense, for Thora has told me all about Norse beliefs. When a Viking warrior dies bravely in battle, if he's lucky, one of Odin's beautiful virgins—the Valkyriers—will bring him to the mansion of the gods, the splendid castle called Valhalla, full of shining shields and glittery swords. He'll eat a banquet of boar and get drunk on mead brimming from horns the Valkyriers hold to his lips. He'll enjoy music and dance and, when the evening ends, he'll be enveloped in the women's charms. The next day, the butchered boar will return to life and the Valkyriers will be virgins anew and the debauchery can begin again.

That last part about the boar and the virgins sounds

very much like a miracle to me, but Thora doesn't seem to feel any need to account for it. She tells me these things as we lie beside each other before sleep, never hesitating over sticky details like resurrection from death.

This island meeting offers everything Viking warriors hope for after death. They're eating boar, listening to music, and buying virgins, all while still on this Earth, still in this life. Viking men who have enough wealth must figure waiting is pointless.

That's why Clay Man didn't let his crew assault us. Business is business, after all.

We are almost back at the tent when Clay Man stops at a dice game. A Norse man rolls a bone die. When it settles, he curses and throws his hands up in anger. He grabs his die and stomps away.

"Sore loser?" says Clay Man to the other Norse gambler.

"We've been at it for a bit," says the man. "And the stakes kept getting higher. He just lost an island to me. He can shout a while about that if he wants. I would too."

"A whole island?" Clay Man rubs his hands together. "I wouldn't mind wagering a bit."

"And what have you got to offer?"

"Silver goods. Enough to win an island."

"Is that so?"

Clay Man takes out a large clay die I watched him make last week. He tosses it in one hand.

"All right, let's have a go."

How foolhardy these northern men are, to gamble away whole islands. All at once I think about how Nuada lost his hand. I turn my eyes away.

Clay Man whoops. He won the first roll. Of course. But within a few rolls, the other man catches on: "That die is weighted."

"Don't be a sore loser," says Clay Man.

"Then use my bone die."

"This is my lucky die," says Clay Man.

"You're lucky, all right." The man stomps over and bumps his chest against Clay Man's. "You're lucky my sword is at the smithy's for repair or I'd challenge you to a *holmganga*."

"A duel on an isolated island—is that what you want? On my island?"

"It's my island, you dirty Russian cheater." The man points both index fingers right in Clay Man's face. "If you dare to gamble again at this festival, I'll have you brought before the assembly of chieftains and demand you be castrated."

Clay Man steps back. "Sore losers, all of you." He pockets his die and leads us away.

We spend a good part of the rest of the day taking down our tent and moving it far from the throngs, far from the dice man. Clay Man grumps continually. He ties us to tent poles for sleep.

+ + +

Clay Man drops the comb in my lap, just like yesterday morning. "Your turn," he says in Norse.

I sit here with my dirty, ratty hair and pick up the comb in my lap and throw it across the tent floor.

Clay Man erupts in a stream of Russian I take to be curses. He shakes his fist in front of my face. I stare at him, surprised. He hasn't threatened me like this before.

"Listen," he says in Norse. "You'll ruin my business looking like that. I won't allow it."

Thora stands behind Clay Man and gives me a pleading look. She's so upset, I think maybe she'll be sick.

Clay Man glares at me. His fist is an empty threat. This is a test of wills. I lift my chin and glare back at him.

Suddenly Clay Man blinks, smiles almost imperceptibly. He swirls around and whacks Thora across the chest so hard, she flies backward and slams on the hard earth. It takes several seconds before she sucks in air again and lets out a whimper.

And I know now: Clay Man was the one who slammed me like that on the ship, when I'd first been stolen—blindfolded and gagged. He was the one who broke my rib. He wouldn't dare slam me now. But he slammed Thora.

I crawl over to the comb and rake slowly at my messy locks. The comb is made of reindeer antler, so it's strong enough to rip open the knots. I don't care if it rips open my scalp.

I swallow and swallow to keep my face from squinching in pain. Thora slowly gets to her feet. She doesn't look at me. We leave the tent.

Overnight many more people have come. A giant market has assembled. Cocks scream in cages under a cloudless, pale blue sky. Thora moves stiffly, wincing. How many ribs did Clay Man crack?

We stop at a tapestry vendor's. The vendor stretches out samples of linen and wool, and women explain the scenes of doomsday tales presided over by gods in radiant blues, greens, yellows. The women wove those tapestries themselves. Clay Man buys a pile and tells the vendor to deliver it to our tent.

When he decides he's paraded us long enough to ensure good business, he brings us back to the tent. It's set up near a field of purple phlox and the tapestries are waiting for us.

Following Clay Man's orders, we drape the largest tapestries over the outside of the tent. Soon ours is the most decorated tent at the festival. Then we go inside. Clay Man uses the remaining tapestries to make a divider within the tent. He tells us to sit behind it, in a line.

I stare through the dim light inside the tent at the reverse side of those tapestries. One has men on horseback with shields in one hand and spears in the other. Eagles fly ahead of them and ravens fly behind them. The other has eagles and wolves feeding on corpses strewn across a battlefield.

It isn't long before we hear footsteps.

"I am Hoskuld." His language tells me he's native Norse for sure.

"Welcome to my tent. I am Gilli."

"Gilli? I've heard of you. They say you're the richest merchant trading here. I suppose you can provide me with anything I might want to buy."

"That depends. What do you want to buy?"

"A *þræll*. A woman. The right kind of woman, that is. If you should happen to have one you can spare."

Clay Man laughs. "You appear to think you've put me on the spot." He laughs again. "Don't be so certain of that." Clay Man lifts the curtain of tapestries. "Take a look."

We twelve sit in a row across the width of the tent. I refuse to look up. I'm seated near the outer side, almost as far from this Viking as I can get.

"That one. She's poorly dressed, but good-looking all the same. Say I wanted to buy her, how much would she cost?"

"Her?" Clay Man's voice is a screech of surprise. He clears his throat. "Three marks of silver."

"Three." The man called Hoskuld sounds taken aback.

"Far too much," says a third voice. One of Hoskuld's companions.

Hoskuld's footsteps come closer. Lord, he stops in front of me. "Three marks of silver is the price of three such þrælar. You value this slave-woman rather highly, it seems."

"You're right. Choose one of the others. For one mark of silver. I'll keep this one."

Hoskuld doesn't move.

"Do you know who he is?" comes the voice of Hoskuld's companion again.

"He gets what he wants," comes the voice of another companion.

"Indeed I do," says Hoskuld.

His tone is deadly. My spine freezes. Who is he, anyway? I look up and meet his eyes. Blue as the hottest flames, with a shock of red hair tumbling down to his shoulders. Everyone knows people with red hair have otherworldly abilities. They say it's lucky to rub the hair of a redheaded child. Hoskuld is no child, though. He's massive and certainly twice my age.

"Here's my purse." Hoskuld keeps his eyes on mine as he talks. "Weigh out the silver in it."

Clay Man lumbers across the tent. He brings out his scales and I hear him unfolding them slowly. Hoskuld finally takes his eyes off me and walks over to Clay Man.

Clay Man sets the measuring pans in place, then he stops abruptly. "Hoskuld, I am an honest man. I don't want to cheat you in this transaction. The woman has a flaw."

"What flaw?"

"She cannot speak."

"Is she deaf?"

"No. She understands—she follows orders. But she's mute. Silent as the stork these feathers came from." He touches the feathers stuck in his hair. "I've tried to get her to speak, but not a word comes from her."

"Finish setting up your scales," says Hoskuld. "Let's see how much my money here weighs."

Clay Man looks at me. In the dark of the tent his eyes glitter like a cat's. His face has gone flaccid. He looks much older—ancient. He puts Hoskuld's silver in one pan. He searches through his clay weights and makes a big show of choosing three. He puts them in the other pan of the scale. "Exactly three marks."

It's more than three marks. Clay Man has chosen some of his heavier weights—the ones he uses when he thinks people are too stupid to know better. But the Viking must have heard what happened yesterday. Surely he wouldn't come into this tent without having asked around first. He must know Clay Man has a reputation for being a cheater. And Clay Man must know that Hoskuld knows.

Of course. Clay Man wants Hoskuld to realize the weights are unfair. That's why he fussed so over choosing the weights. It's his only chance of getting out of the deal. Of keeping me.

Hoskuld touches his fingertips to the clay weights. But he doesn't pick them up. "The bargain is sealed, then," he says at last. "You take the silver and I will take the woman."

The men shake hands. Clay Man doesn't look at me.

Hoskuld rubs his hands together and gives a satisfied smile. "You surprise me, Gilli. I must say you acted uncommonly fairly in not trying to trick me into a purchase."

"I'm an honest man."

Hoskuld grins and his ruddy cheeks appear monster-like. "And those are correct weights, I suppose?"

"For this *þræll*, yes."

One of Hoskuld's companions harrumphs.

Clay Man turns his back on them and moves closer to Hoskuld. "You paid the just price for this one. She's special."

Hoskuld laughs now. "I suppose Russia must produce some honest folk. After all, our own god Odin came from Russia. From Asgard, on the River Tanais."

"Not far from my home," says Clay Man.

"Those stork feathers in your hair, do they come with the woman?"

Clay Man steps back. He hesitates.

"Our god Hoenir is long-legged." Hoskuld pushes his hair back and looks penetratingly at Clay Man. "Some say he's a stork. He gave man memory. Throw in those feathers, and I'll remember you. Don't throw them in, and I'll still remember you. Differently."

The threat hangs in the air. Clay Man pulls the feathers out and thrusts them at the Viking. Hoskuld goes over to one of his companions and hands him the feathers.

While his back is turned, Clay Man reaches inside his shirt and pulls out the leather strap from which my gold teething ring hangs. He quickly tosses it onto my lap. I immediately tuck it into one of the pockets I've sewn inside my tunic. My heart races. I can't fathom why Clay Man would give me this parting gift, and I don't care why—I'm just glad to have it.

Hoskuld comes near and leans over me. He is tall and his tunic leaves one arm free, giving me the strange sense that he is off balance.

He reaches out his hand and closes it around mine. He pulls me to my feet and leads me away.

PART THREE

CHAPTER SEVENTEEN:
DERED M-BETHO

This is a tent. There's a world outside it. But I'm inside.

The body near me, this man Hoskuld, smells of apple. He ate meat and minced onion porridge for dinner, followed by apple tarts and a cake with cloves and raisins. All of that was after he had already partaken of the pig roasted on a spit outside. He has a formidable appetite.

He talks. He keeps asking me if I'm really mute, or just playing a game. He asked me this as he led me from Clay Man's tent. He asked me this several times during the evening meal. In quiet tones. He has faith in persistence.

He asks now.

He puts his hands on me.

I could cry out. I could beg for mercy. I have never spoken Norse out loud, but in my head there are so many things to say.

But I won't speak. This man may never come to believe I'm an enchantress. He doesn't ask anything of that sort. He gives no evidence of thinking my silence is anything but defect or determination. I don't know what he did with the stork feathers. But I do know my silence intrigues him.

Besides, he is an animal. Brigid taught me, you don't talk to animals. You keep your mouth shut and watch them. That's exactly what she said. Hush, hush. Then they know you're not going to hurt them.

But they can still hurt you.

The vipers circle. They come in for the kill.

His hands find my roundness. Things that were mine, my personal treasures. Things that made me feel pretty. That amazed me when they grew. That made me glad to be a woman. These were part of a clean me, hidden in my tunic, waiting for me to share them with the one I would choose.

Choice is an illusion.

As is cleanliness. I grow filthy both inside and out now. And none of that filth bothers him. All my efforts to appear witchy, all to no end. He actually smoothed my hair after the evening meal. Smoothed it, as though he were kind and not the beast he is. And he promised to buy me beautiful gems to adorn my hair. He called me exquisite. He said I deserved the best.

Does he think he's the best?

He moans. His hands squeeze. His mouth demands.

It wasn't all that long ago that I was home. Less than a half year, I would guess, though I have no real sense of time anymore. The seasons here are so different. The light goes on so long. I'm always disoriented.

My tunic comes off easily. I am totally without defense. Unsafe.

Safety is another illusion. I should have given it up long ago. When Brigid and I were taken. When she jumped into the freezing river. An eight-year-old, alone. Safety. Am I a fool, that I didn't surrender such childish ideas then?

He breathes on me. Heavy, wet breath. He drank enough to be dead drunk, but he seems far from that. His eyes are clear, despite that opaque breath.

If I had a knife like the one he tucks in his belt, I could cut his breath into blocks and beat him over the head with them. But my hands are empty. And his knife is in the corner of the tent, on the pile of his clothes.

He leaves the knife there as though I will not think of stabbing him. He walked beside me all afternoon, all evening, with the knife at his side, so close to my hand. Can he be so naive as to believe that I do not harbor him ill will in this act? Can his thoughts be as thick as his breath?

But I won't pick up the knife. I won't lose my soul to hatred.

All I can do is breathe deeply of him. Breathe and hope that his vapors will poison me. He is venomous, after all. Let the poison enter my lungs, seal away all my words, all my songs, forever.

I never was good at singing. My voice couldn't hold a tune right. It was Nuada, my brother, who could make even the birds stop their trilling to listen to him. But I had songs in my heart. I did. Once I did.

His hands are calloused. They hurt the tender parts of me. Has he done hard labor himself? But I know already that he is wealthy. I've seen the men who work in his service. He's respected, and in this country it's riches that make people respect you. And he's feared. Clay Man didn't dare go against him. He bought me just like that. Without a second thought. So I know he's done it before. He probably has many þrælar. And he probably doesn't recognize that any of them are human. Maybe he's like the man who led the two þrælar up into the hills outside Hyllestad to bury his treasure. Maybe this Hoskuld has murdered þrælar, like you might kill a rat. No, not a rat. A rat marauds in your grains. But þrælar only work. They work and work and work. So it would be like killing a dog—a loyal dog, who has stood by you all his life.

Maybe I'll be lucky and he'll kill me. Death is the only possible escape for me now.

His hair leaps from his head in flames. To think, I once looked at red hair as lucky. My skin blisters.

He's on me, pressing down so hard, I'll break. If only I would break. He's splitting me in two. But I don't want to be two pieces. I want to shatter. Thousands of little pieces of me. They could blow away in the wind. Gone.

Because I am gone. This isn't me. This can't be me. *Athir*—Father—where are you? *Du-mem-se*—protect me. Like Brigid whispered, maybe in her sleep.

But there is no me to protect.

I am no more.

I've been eradicated *trí drochgnímu*—through evil deeds.

But at least they're not my own deeds. I didn't cause this. I couldn't have caused this. Nothing I've ever done merits this. Not even failing to hold on to Brigid, that most terrible thing.

Oh, Lord. You've shown me *dered m-betho*—the end of the world.

Whatever became of mercy?

CHAPTER EIGHTEEN:
SACRIFICE

We're standing in a grove under evening sun. The grove is far enough away from the marketplace that we cannot hear its music and confusion. Out here quiet reigns. A circle of huge stones encompasses the grove. People have gathered here to worship, invited by a small group of free men, the most important being the great chieftain Hoskuld. My master. It's a sacrifice ceremony, to ensure the success of the journey ahead for Hoskuld and his companions. We are to return to the land he and his companions came from, with all the *þrælar* and supplies they have bought.

The yeoman farmers of this town on Brännö Island are participating. They have rights *þrælar* don't have: They carry weapons, and can take part in the voting assembly, and now will be part of this ceremony. As far as I can tell, it's opportunistic on their part. They don't need to invoke the blessings of the gods; they aren't the ones about to make the long sea journey. They aren't even friends of Hoskuld or any of the other free men making the journey. They've lined up their wooden, carved wagons and they wait for the feast that will follow the ceremony—that's the reason they're here. It's their chance to be hosted for once, to eat at others' expense. Their children play in scattered groups. The little ones make toy piggies by sticking wood legs on pinecones. The big ones jump hopscotch and chase one another on stilts.

"What animal do you think we should sacrifice? It's your choice." Hoskuld puts his finger on the center of my cheek.

I look away.

He runs it down my jaw, down my neck, down . . .

I flinch.

"Come on, Beauty. After these last few nights, we're past that. Or we should be."

He calls me Beauty. Mother said I had become a beauty. It was one of the last things she ever said to me. I wish I could strike his tongue mute.

"Tell me what to sacrifice," he says. "A horse? An ox? A pig? We need some luck. Let's get Njord on our side."

Njord is the god of ships and of wealth. When Thora told me that, I wanted to laugh. The two are connected, of course. Vikings get so much of their wealth from jumping into ships and raiding the rest of the world.

Hoskuld kisses me on the cheek. His breath is mead gone sour. "It's a long voyage to Iceland, after all."

Iceland. The place we're going to now has a name. Iceland. It means nothing to me. I will go to Iceland in the luxurious blue gown I'm now wearing.

The morning after our first night together, Hoskuld bathed me with his own hands. He washed my hair. He patted me dry. He did it all slowly, almost gingerly, as if I were a child that he must take care not to be rough with.

Then he opened a chest in his tent. It was full of beautiful smallclothes—underclothes—and dresses and cloaks. He told me to pick the ones I wanted. "These aren't gifts," he said. "You never give gifts to *prælar*, because then the objects become cursèd trash. This is a necessity. Your other clothes were rags. But to be fair to Gilli, it's easier for me to clothe one *præll* than for him to clothe a dozen."

Hoskuld's companions say I look stunning in this dress. Irish women are as good at spinning as Norse women. Better maybe, because Irish women use spinning wheels, which assures uniformity of thickness, while Norse women spin by hand with a stick and spindle. They have to soak the wool in fermented urine and hot water to make it more workable.

But when it comes to weaving, Norse women are superior. Sometimes they stand at vertical looms. But often they use small tablets that allow them to make more intricate designs, even with wool. Thora tried to teach me once; it's hard. The linen of this dress is blue like the deepest sea. It falls to my feet in soft pleats, unhindered by a belt. Scarlet silk threads and brown horsehair threads pattern all the edges in swirls interlaced with knots. The woven hair band that goes with it is scarlet and brown with blue patterns. The tailor had a good eye. I'm impressed with heathen sensibility and skill at cloth. Norsemen obviously do not fear spirits in colors on their women.

Hoskuld's wife will know this dress was supposed to have been hers. She'll know immediately from the patterns. They are the same as on the other dresses in the chest—the ones he'll give to her, I'm sure.

On my shoulders is a woolly mantle lined with very fine squirrel fur that peeks out around the edge of the hood. Hoskuld placed it on me. There is no other mantle with a hood in the chest—no other mantle meant for a woman.

His wife will have so many reasons for hating me. I am going on a journey to Iceland, where I will be hated.

We've been preparing for the journey all along. Hoskuld spends his days ordering his other þrælar around. He has accumulated many recently. A few children. Several young, strong people.

I wanted to lead him back to Clay Man's tent to buy Thora. Our fates may be awful, but at least there would be comfort in sharing them. I couldn't get him to go that way, though. When I tugged on his arm, he said, "You'll have to speak if you want me to go somewhere." He touched my lips. "Speak, Beauty, and I'll go wherever you say." But I will not speak. Maybe I no longer even know how to.

So Thora is gone from me forever. All her energy and enthusiasm, gone.

Hoskuld also bought an older woman—a hunched-over soul with a lazy eye, who claims to have particular skills with medicinal herbs.

He tells his new *þrælar* to buy salted and smoked meats, dried cod and vegetables and fruits, crushed grain, juniper berries, and any other herbs Lazy Eye wants in case someone gets sick. These things are packed into wooden barrels and boxes and stacked inside his tent.

All Hoskuld's *þrælar* work. All but me. I simply adorn his arm. And fill his bed.

He gathers not just food, but tools. Forge tongs, pincers, adzes, awls, hammers. Oh, yes, hammers. He picked up one of them, pinned me against a stone wall, and slammed the hammer on the stone beside my cheek. It gave off a spark. "Almost as good as Mjollnir," he said with a smile. Mjollnir is the name of Thor's magic hammer that he uses to fight the frost giants.

I don't know if Hoskuld realizes the full effect of his threats. He wants me to fear him, but I doubt he wants me to hate him. He kissed me before he let me go, and his kiss seemed happy. He adores good tools. Yesterday we stood by an iron smith, watching while the man hardened ax heads over a fire. Hoskuld bought ten regular axes, ten two-headed ones, and ten broad-blade ones.

And a sword with a hilt of walrus ivory decorated in geometric designs of gold, copper, and black niello. Hoskuld handled it with reverence.

After he bought it, he told me, "This never should have been for sale in the first place. Swords like this get passed down through families. Respect for families is second only to respect for the gods." He put his finger on the center of my cheek when he said "respect for families." That was the first time he did that, but he's done it many times since.

And he bought a dozen simpler swords with wood grips covered in leather. And some two-edged swords. And bows and arrows. And metal helmets.

He's going to turn his crew into an army at this rate.

The battle scenes in the tapestries that covered Clay Man's tent come back to me. Wolves chewing on men's thighs; eagles pecking out entrails.

But other things he buys are harmless, clearly gifts.

Bearskin hats. Skates of cow bones to tie to shoes, for gliding over ice in the winter. Toy axes of bronze and toy wooden swords and shields. And a cowhide ball for kicking on the ice. He told me there's a midwinter feast called Yule, in honor of Frey. The adults pray to the god for a good harvest the next year, while the children kick balls on the ice.

Somewhere in Iceland children wait for him. Young children, because Thora told me that by the time a child is twelve he uses a real sword.

Hoskuld buys gifts for his wife, too. Pottery and fine silver jewelry and a tortoiseshell brooch.

They will all hate me. The wife, especially. How could she not? A household of hate.

And he's been gathering men for the trip. He interrogates each one. Many have come from huge distances, catching rides on fishing boats, boats shuttling wood, boats collecting eggs or down feathers for quilts from birds that nest on deserted islands. Difficult passages. It took some of them weeks to travel here.

I listen as Hoskuld interviews them. And I listen later as they talk among themselves. They leave behind famine and poverty. Some leave behind extortion—either as victims or as perpetrators in fear of being caught. And some just leave behind personal pain, for these ones are misshapen or have a strange gait or peer out from haunted eyes. They are shunned at home as magicians or witches. They're tired of being beggars and tramps. Hoskuld is building a crew of the miserable and the deviant, who will never see their homes again and never want to.

Maybe that's what it takes to emigrate. I would never have left my home by choice. Despair envelops me. Like them, I will never see my home again.

I look at these unfortunates—these are the people who will wield the weapons Hoskuld has been accumulating. But at least the *prælar* won't be going into battle. I heard someone say it's illegal for *prælar* to bear arms.

"Are you listening to me?" Hoskuld puts his arm around my waist. I am jolted back to the present. I look around at all the people gathered for this sacrifice. "Don't get lost inside that beautiful head." Hoskuld puts his mouth to my ear. "I know you hear me. I watch your shoulders tighten as I come up from behind. Your hearing is perfect. And I know you understand. Your face speaks your reactions to my words. You can't fool me." His grip on my rib cage tightens. "Choose the animal for sacrifice, Beauty. You could even choose a *præll*."

A *præll*?

Me, I think. Please sacrifice me. I look up at the sky. Take me, Lord.

An eagle soars overhead.

"Are you crazy?" Hoskuld steps away from me. "We never sacrifice eagles. Odin can take on the guise of an eagle. His wife, Frigg, can appear as a falcon. They're sacred."

I blink. Is everyone outside of Eire insane when it comes to birds? Do they all see them as something else in disguise?

"But if you want a bird, we can do a cock," says Hoskuld. "It won't be enough, though. Not for this long a voyage. So we'll do an ox as well. I like watching them bury ox bones after a feast. It makes the earth strong."

He walks away. He expects me to follow, I know.

A seagull shrieks. A brown bird chases it. It's smaller than the seagull, with white and brown bands across its tail. How does a smaller bird get up the gumption to chase a seagull?

Hoskuld stops and looks back over his shoulder.

I glance again at that determined brown bird. Brigid and Maeve and Thora—three small birds who never quit. And here I am, a stork, a giant of birds. I must not quit. Deep inside, I must keep my spirit alive and fighting. No matter what the nights are like. Quitting would be disloyal to their memories.

I follow Hoskuld.

CHAPTER NINETEEN:
ATTACK

We're onboard the middle ship of three. I'm excited to be on a ship again. It's strange, but somehow just being onboard makes me feel like I know what I'm doing.

I still don't have any idea where Iceland is, but I don't care. We're going to a new world.

All three ships are knorrs, the largest ships I've ever seen. They had this one out of the water to check it over before the journey. I walked the length of its shadow. Ninety steps. And twenty steps across. A long, slender ship, indeed.

Hoskuld walked around the beached ship as well. He gave final whacks to nails here and there. He used his favorite hammer. He checked rivets. "The metal for these nails and rivets was smelted from bog iron," he said. He's taken to explaining things to me, like Thora used to.

When he said that, I thought of Irish bogs. Of that crazy mare that got stuck. Of how Brigid lured her out. I went blind. But Hoskuld was too busy to notice. In the last few days before they pushed the ship over rolling logs out into the water, he rushed constantly, so much so that he ignored me. Except at night.

He oversaw every detail. He had tar-dipped wool jammed between boards to keep out water and add flexibility. The ribs and twisted bands in the frame are naturally shaped roots and branches of spruce and pine; they, too, are known for flex. He said, "No storm can destroy a ship that gives with the force of the waves."

I don't want to think about storms. Right now the water is calm. The sun shines fantastically bright. The wind is steady but soft. It fills the gigantic, square, woolen sail that protrudes over the ship sides and reaches three-quarters of the way up the towering mast. Ropes from its corners attach to the prow and sides.

The mast is in the center. There's no deck around it. The deep bottom of the boat is open to the air there. A layer of fodder covers it, and a lone cow stands immobilized by the swell and fall of the sea. The smells of fodder and sea mix in a funny, pleasant way.

The decks at the front and the back of the ship are of oak planks wider than my foot is long. Pine planks make up the hull. All the planks were split from the center of a trunk, so each has the same grain and reacts the same at sea. They're made from green wood with no knots, no gnarly points that resist. Every measurement was taken by eye.

234

Hoskuld's voice rang with pride as he pointed out these things before we set sail. His eyes searched my face as he told me that last fact. He wanted to see if I showed the surprise of a foreigner. He wants to know where I come from. I feel his eyes on me always; he's fascinated.

But I deny him any satisfaction I can. I work hard to make my face less loquacious. I think of other things when he questions me. Thora. Two days ago I saw Clay Man pass with only four virgins at his heels. Someone bought Thora. In my head I become a stork. I glide to Thora and she climbs on my back. We rise on warm winds. No harm can come to her.

And Hoskuld is determined that no harm will come to his ships. Fifteen sea chests line the length of each side. When the wind lulls, men with arms nearly the size of my waist sit on the chests and row. Now, though, with the sail billowing, the men have pulled in the oars and closed the wooden flaps over the holes to seal out the sea. They are busy bailing water, bucket after bucket, muscles flexing. A shield is mounted above every oarlock.

More shields are mounted starboard. And a large sack of stones sits near the rudder. As we sail, it's moved around for balance. Hoskuld says the cargo under the front and rear decks can be moved around too, if necessary.

These three ships are of equal size. The front one

carries fifty people. The rear one holds fewer because it also carries timber. Our ship holds only thirty, since the open area around the mast is much larger on ours. But ours has the most terrifying prow: a dragon head with a gaping mouth—a firedrake. The gold paint glints menacingly in the sun. I can see that only if I lean out near the front. But I know, because I stood in awe beneath it the day before we launched. I noticed everything and committed it all to memory.

That's when Hoskuld went to King Hakon to pay his respects. I walked behind him into the king's tent.

"And, so, Hoskuld, you wait till you are about to sail before you visit me?"

Hoskuld squirmed and I was glad: Someone had power over him, after all. "I had to oversee everything. You know how the success of a voyage depends on the details."

"That can be true," said the king. He looked at me. "And who is this?"

"My Beauty."

"I'd like to come home to a woman that fine."

Hoskuld's neck turned the color of his hair. "When you come to Iceland, I will host you grandly."

My stomach became a ball of ice. Did Hoskuld intend me to be a part of such hosting?

"Indeed? Then I might come soon."

"Not too soon," said Hoskuld. "Iceland has few trees, so my farmhouse is made of sod and turf and whatever driftwood I came across. I'd like to build a better one before you come."

"Timber, is that what you're after? I'll have a ship loaded with building timber for a new house, one good enough to host a king."

Hoskuld grinned. "An exceptional gift. Thank you, my king."

"And here." King Hakon went to a chest. He gave Hoskuld a heavy gold ring and an ornate sword.

"Your generosity astounds me. I am humbled with the honor of carrying this sword." Hoskuld didn't tell the king that he'd already bought a sword even more highly decorated than this one. And I was glad, so very glad, to see Hoskuld lying because another had such power over him.

But then, later that night, Hoskuld whispered to me in bed. "Kings are expected to be generous. That's how they lead. That's how they inspire and buoy up the spirits of their men." He kissed my throat. "And that's how their men wind up richer and richer. We now have a third ship, and it's full of timber." So Hoskuld had had the better of King Hakon, after all.

We started out this first day hugging the shore, passing much smaller fishing vessels and levy ships and coastal boats of various sorts with only a few men on them. So many boats. Every Norseman must own at least one.

As evening comes, we anchor the ships together near a beach. A clamorous noise comes from the prow of the ship I'm on. Everyone laughs. I see now a cage with three large ravens inside, cawing and jumping about frenetically. No one raises ravens. Are they here for ceremonial purposes?

But my curiosity disappears as the excitement of land hits me. All the people rush off the ships. The children run. The adults chatter in relief to be on land again. Someone talks about what an easy day it was, and how very different it will be when we go days at sea without seeing land on any side.

At those words, a *þræll* cries out his terror of dying at sea.

Instantly Hoskuld's arm swings and catches the man on the back of the head with a dull thud.

The *þræll* goes flying. He's caught by two others. All the *þrælar* huddle together and stare at the ground.

"No complaints," booms Hoskuld. "Not a one. Look at me." The men look up. Hoskuld shakes his hammer fist in the air. "Not a one."

Everyone goes about their business.

But I grab Hoskuld by the arm and glare at him.

"What? You object?" The corner of his mouth twitches, as though he finds me amusing. He puts his face to mine. "It's a question of morale. Don't worry yourself about things you don't understand."

Oh, I understand. I've had too many lessons in brutality. I do not lower my gaze.

He runs a finger along my jawline. "Clenched teeth? What have we here? A rebellion? Do not cross me, Beauty." He puts his mouth to my ear. "Especially when others are watching," he growls. He pulls free and walks away.

When my heart stops banging, I walk to join two women *þrælar*, but they quickly move away. No one wants to be aligned with someone who crossed Hoskuld. I stand alone and look around.

A tripod of overlapping iron poles, collapsed for transport, now appears, with a big black pot hanging from it. It reminds me of Clay Man's scales. The simple cleverness of the design impresses me against my will. We cook a fish stew and eat hearty.

One of Hoskuld's men tells the saga of Sigurd Fafnesbane. There are a few parts I don't understand, because Thora never told me this tale. But I gather that it's about a gold treasure that once belonged to a dwarf. Everyone is mesmerized.

I move close to Hoskuld to listen. Maybe he'll say something to help me understand better. But he takes my nearness the wrong way. He throws his arm around me and pulls me tight to him. He strokes my cheek and rests his own on the top of my head. "It's okay, Beauty. I forgive you." I stiffen, but he gives no sign of noticing.

Toward noon of the second day we leave the shore behind and head southwest through open water. I can't help but swallow worries. Without natural landmarks to guide us, how can we not get lost? But we soon reach islands. It's early evening.

Hoskuld says to a man, "The ravens." That's all. But the man runs and wraps the cage of ravens with several blankets. I watch, uncomprehending.

We anchor offshore, as close as possible to the easternmost island. The free men gather in small groups. Something's up. I listen; someone will surely say where we are. But no one's speaking. It's as though they've all decided everything ahead of time. Men from the first ship grab spears and brightly painted shields with metal domes in the center. They go on land.

The rest of us wait, watching the shore. I hear no sounds of battle. Nothing. Except now the honking of geese. And high-pitched screams. The men appear on the shore, running, behind a group of children, chasing a flock of domesticated geese. They throw the children and birds into the first boat. Each boat rotates the sail and sets the rudder and we're off again immediately. With a slew of new *þrælar*. What do parents do when their children simply disappear? How do they go on living?

That night I cry. Hoskuld says in bewilderment, "You cry now? After being with me for nearly three weeks? Now?" It doesn't occur to the man that someone could cry for another's pain. Or maybe he truly doesn't understand that *þrælar* have pain.

Thora told me that in the north country *húskarls*—farmhands, who are free men but hardly better off than *þrælar*—sometimes give up their children willingly to slave traders because they don't have enough food to go around. Some even leave their newborns out in the snow when they can't feed them. So maybe Hoskuld doesn't understand anything. Maybe he sees that and cannot guess the way those sacrifices slice through a parent's innards. Maybe he is hopelessly stupid rather than brutally cruel. But does the difference matter?

As if to answer my thoughts, he holds my face in the cup of his palms and croons to me. His lips soften. His limpid eyes turn gentle. In this moment he seems like a man who could have been good if he'd lived in another world—in a world with angels. I could almost be comforted by those eyes, I could almost stop crying.

We sleep on the deck under countless stars, a fiery inscription on the sky. And I know others cry too. I can't not know that.

In the morning I wake to raven caws. Someone removed the blankets from the cage, so their noises come loud and clear. They're frantic again.

I stand and find our three ships hugging a new shore, this time on the port side. But the men are not forming groups—there seems to be no plan to raid, thank heavens. From the path of the sun, I realize we're heading south. As the day passes, I stand at the prow and actually enjoy the spray of the water. There was a sun shower around noon, but it cleared quickly and the air has warmed up nicely. Everyone's taken off their cloaks and folded them into a pile.

Hoskuld comes up beside me. He hands me a tiny spoon. "Clean my ears."

I remove his earwax. I did this the night before we first set sail, too. That time I wondered how much pressure it would take to shove this little wooden spoon into his brain. I wondered if it would break, and I feared that only that possibility stopped me. But this time I clean him without mental flights of violence. I am cleaning him, nothing more, nothing less. No moment seems more or less than it is.

Now he hands me tweezers. I remove stray hairs above his beard, long hairs from his nose and ears.

"Don't you want to know why you're making me handsome? Tonight we attack Inis Eoghain."

My breath catches. Inis Eoghain is the peninsula on the very northern tip of Eire. I had thought we were far from my home.

"Wish me luck?" Hoskuld laughs. "Look." He points to the red flag with a black raven in the center. He attached it to the mast a little while ago. "The raven is Thor's holy bird. See how it flutters? That means we'll have victory." He chucks me under the neck. "I'm cautious. I never attack when the flag droops. And I've never yet faced defeat."

He unties the flag and puts it away in the box he took it from before. I catch a glimpse of feathers. He keeps the three stork feathers he got from Clay Man with that flag! I would want to know why, but right now my head swirls. We're going to Inis Eoghain. I had given up all hope of escape long ago. But now . . .

The next instant everything changes. Hoskuld orders the men to lower the sail. What's going on?

The three ships bob about on the open water. We eat flat bread while the sails flap loudly and the masts creak.

It will be time to open our cache of dried and pickled foods soon. This bread finishes off everything fresh that we brought with us.

A man goes to the side of the boat and stares into the water. He holds a long spear with three prongs ending in barbs and a rope attached to the handle. I walk over beside him and look down at a thick, shimmering school of anchovies. What good would a spear be on such small fish?

The geese in the first boat set up a clatter.

From nowhere vast flocks of cormorants fill the air. The noisy birds dive for the fish. The geese seem to be egging them on.

When the cormorants leave, schools of herring come. They pass in and out of the ships, as though curious about who we might be. They are so many that the waters look silver.

Suddenly they race off. A huge tuna chases them. The man shouts and throws the spear. Four more men rush up, and they tug on the rope attached to the spear. They haul the heavy fish onto the deck.

Why, they knew that tuna was coming. These people know more about the sea than even the Irish. They may be brutish, but they are also clever.

We tie the three ships together, side by side, and feast

on stewed tuna, everyone eating the same—even the
þrælar. I haven't yet figured out what rules distinguish
þrælar from free men and free men from the leaders. But
in this moment, I hardly care; the tuna is rich and dark
and meaty. The smell is so clean, my nostrils flare. People
talk in little groups, happy to be filling their bellies.

As am I. A full belly encourages a heart that had too
quickly accepted a horrible fate. I must be strong and
alert. If any opportunity for escape presents itself, I must
act swiftly.

Dusk finally oozes over the surface of the water. We
set sail. Of course: We'll attack under the cover of night.
That's in my favor. It is easier to disappear in the dark,
especially in a blue dress.

Men stand on the deck and hold the round shields.
They make a wall in front of them by overlapping the
edges. Other men try to kick through. Oh, they're
practicing—a dry run. When the wall withstands the
affront, they clap each other on the back in congratulations. Then they take down the sails and we row.

Rowing is much slower than sailing. But I understand: a ship is easier to spot with the sail up.

The rocky shores loom close in the weak moonlight. This is my country. Eire. Dearest Eire, asleep and
unsuspecting.

We anchor in a small cove and the ravens scream. A man quickly blankets their cage again, until no sound is heard. The three ships come together so close that men jump easily from one to the other, as they gather their gear and discuss plans for the raid. Some of the men will be ready for a fight; others will have their arms free to carry the loot.

I stay out of the way. Let them leave. Hurry. Go. Then I'll jump over the side: Brigid's lesson.

Hoskuld and his companions are going on this attack. They lay out all the contingencies together.

"But remember," says one of the men, "react to the moment. If things go wrong, forget the plans, and just do what's best at the moment."

"Right," says another. "No one is in charge."

"Or everyone is," says a third.

Hoskuld beams. "That's how it's done in Iceland—so that's how it's done on a ship headed for Iceland."

The men embrace.

Hoskuld told me it would be this way. He said a chief is more a mediator than a ruler. But I didn't believe him. I thought he wouldn't be able to put aside his need to dominate. I see now that I was wrong. Hoskuld does what needs to be done. He is versatile and agile—physically, mentally, emotionally.

There are things about Vikings I could come to admire, if only their strengths weren't used to bully the whole rest of the world.

The men put on suits of chain mail. Hoskuld comes over to me. "Lift an arm. Go ahead."

I lift one arm of the chain mail. It's remarkably heavy. I can't understand how anyone can move inside it.

"Wrought-iron links. Don't you worry about me, Beauty. It took a master smith a year to make this suit. I won't get cut, no matter what." He opens a wooden box and takes out an ax that's larger than the others I've seen. He smiles. "It takes two hands to wield this. If anyone gets in my way, he won't be there for long."

I step back.

"Wait." Hoskuld puts down the ax. "Come here." He lifts me off my feet and carries me like a small child, draped across his arms. He reeks of sweat. He practiced in the shield drill as hard as anyone. "Did you really think I'd leave you untied without me here? You're too beautiful to risk losing. And too mysterious." He jumps with me down into the bottom of the ship and ties me to the base of the mast.

I don't kick or thrash. What's the point? He'd only beat me down. I sink into the soft fodder up to my ankles. And just as quickly as defeat came, hope rises again:

I will act sweet, for if he thinks I'm docile, he might get sloppy on his return and untie me before we are too far from shore for me to jump overboard.

"Listen, *þrælar*," Hoskuld shouts. "That land out there is full of madmen. They'll kill you as soon as look at you. They hate you. They hate everyone who isn't one of them. So forget thoughts of escape." He holds his arm out straight and points his finger, for all the world as threatening as a sword. "And if this *þræll* is gone when I come back, all of you die." He looks at me, then he looks back at them. "If anyone hurts her, all of you will wish you'd died."

They are *þrælar* themselves. They believe him. I believe him.

248

CHAPTER TWENTY:
ONION

A sheep bleats in my ear. I must have fallen asleep, they were gone so long. How stupid of me. Now I struggle to my feet, working the rope up the mast as I stand. Sheep are tumbling into the fodder. The startled cow lows piteously. From down in the basin of the boat it's hard to see much, but through the fuzzy dawn I make out men climbing into the ship with sheep draped across their shoulders. They plop them into this area, sometimes on top of one another. From their pungent odor I can tell these creatures just had their second shearing of the season.

A man jumps in and pushes me down out of the way, and three together pull on the ropes to raise the sail. No one's untying me. I'm stuck. We're moving already. Leaving Eire.

A girl screams and screams. I can't see her past the frantic sheep, but she's got to be near. On this ship. The screams come closer, until she's thrown down next to me.

"I'll get free, you wretched Vikings!" Good Ulster

Gaelic. The sound reverberates inside my head. I am so glad to hear it. Tears blur my vision.

And an immediate question: Does she know what happened at Downpatrick that night? Can she tell me who lives still? Is my family safe? I smile at her.

That's all it takes. She rushes me, ramming headfirst into my belly. Her fist comes up from below and slams me in the throat. I cough blood.

"A real minx, that's what you are," comes a man's voice in Norse. I manage to turn my head and see he's caught her from behind. He ties her hands.

We set sail, and here I am, still tied to the mast. *Tocad*—luck—where has luck gone? How could I be so unlucky as to be ripped from my homeland a second time?

Someone finally unties me and drags me up to the deck. I stand unsteadily, holding on to a tall coil of rope for support, and look out toward the land—my Eire. People crowd on the shore and shoot arrows at us. Not a single one hits, we're already out of range. Too far to swim. I sink to the deck floor, dig my fingers into my hair, and rock back and forth. I am defeated, exhausted, undone.

Someone drops a flat bread on my lap. I thought they were all finished. I look up in confusion. It's Lazy Eye. Before she was on the third ship, but somehow she's been moved to this one.

"Help me," she says in Norse. "And I'll help you."

How could a *þræll* from the north country help me? And what does she want of me? I have no more power than she does. I gnaw on the bread and stare at her through the dim light.

Now I see them. Four. Four wounded men. Lazy Eye gives rapid orders. A woman *þræll* washes a wounded man with seawater. Another strikes the fire stones and starts a flame under a pot, feeding it excrement from our waste pots. Another sharpens a knife on a slipstone. And two children go from wounded man to wounded man, giving them beer.

Lazy Eye mixes herbs in a bowl, pounding them into a paste with whale oil. The sharp minty odor of betony reaches me. "Finish that bread, finish, finish," she hisses over at me. "Then help with the beer. Hurry."

Whether it is the bread or the surprise of being needed, I do not know, but from somewhere I find energy. I tuck the rest of the flatbread inside my smallclothes under this dress and fill a horn with beer.

"That one." Lazy Eye points to the man whose side gushes blood. "He's first."

The children have stayed away from him. So have the women. He hasn't even been washed yet. That much blood frightens all of us. I try to get the man to drink, but he throws his head from side to side. I splash the beer over his open wound. He screams.

"Good," says Lazy Eye. "You know what cleans wounds. Good."

For a moment enough blood was washed away that I could see a white part of his insides. But now it gushes red again.

Lazy Eye holds the sharpened knife in the fire a moment. Then she has two men *þrælar* pin down the bleeding man while she presses the hot knife somewhere inside him. He screams. She cuts away the smallest amount of skin around the edges of his wound now. He's still screaming. She nods to me and I pour more beer. She packs moss into the wound, then pulls a threaded needle from her bodice and sews his muscles together. He screams and screams and passes out. She sews while I drizzle beer over the wound.

"This is taking too long." Lazy Eye looks over at another man, who's sitting and moaning over a battered leg. "I have to set that bone before that one's leg swells too much. You finish." She gives me the needle and thread.

I will my trembling hands to be still. The blood has stopped gushing, but it still oozes. The sticky sweetness turns my innards. I stitch carefully.

By the time I finish, Lazy Eye is at my side again. The man with the broken leg has neat splints around it and is already asleep from so much beer. Another has a clean linen bandage around his arm and the third around the top of his head. I marvel at Lazy Eye's efficiency.

She mumbles approval at my uneven stitching and smears the rest of her herbal paste over it all. Then she bandages my patient. From around her neck she takes a leather pouch. She opens the drawstring and picks out a polished stone amulet. She lifts the man's head and puts it on him. I know about protective amulets. People wear them to keep away harm. What good can they do after harm has already been inflicted? Norsemen must have different ideas. I hope she's right.

He may have killed Irish men. But he's hurt. So helpless. I say a prayer for him inside my head.

Lazy Eye whispers magic words over him. Then she turns to me. "I'm Torild." She pats my hand approvingly.

It's full morning now. And I'm more tired than I've ever been before. I rest my back against a wooden chest and sleep.

✦ ✦ ✦

Onion fills the air. My eyes open. A child holds a bowl of onion porridge under my nose. "Feed this to the sick man. The witch says."

I take the porridge and kneel beside the man from last night. His eyes are glassy bright and his cheeks are flushed. I put a small spoonful in his mouth. He looks at me vaguely and swallows. I feed him slowly. I'm afraid to touch his skin; I'm afraid it's hot.

After a few mouthfuls, he blinks. His eyes grow sharp. "Onion? This is onion." A muscle in his cheek twitches. "Tell her I smell like sweat."

I don't know what he's talking about. He doesn't seem delirious, though. But he's clearly upset. I nod.

"Promise. I don't want to drown. I'd rather die on the deck where the Valkyriers can find me and bring me to Valhalla. Or Freya. I'd go with Freya to Folkvang, too. Anything but drowning. Have pity. It's a simple lie. Promise."

I'm confused, but I nod again. What else can I do?

He lets me feed him the rest of the porridge. Then he falls into a feverish sleep.

Hoskuld comes up to me as I make the man more comfortable. It's the first time I've seen him since the raid. "I missed you last night," he says loudly. "Your sweet taste. I've grown accustomed to you, Beauty."

Anyone can hear. I feel myself blushing even as I try to make my face stone.

"Want to see what we got? A casket of precious

metals and reliquaries. The Irish are dumb and predict-able. Every monastery is the same. It's as though they package up gifts for us. The jewels are spectacular."

Ill-gotten riches. They should bring a curse down on his head.

"I'll let you choose something beautiful," he says warmly. "Whatever you want, it's yours."

A gift for a *þræll*? Something has changed.

He takes my hand and pulls me over to the casket. I stare down at the loot. Delicate gold chains and bracelets. Engraved silver cups and bowls. Dazzling jeweled books. Anyone could recognize the superior Irish craftsman-ship. I don't want stolen jewelry. I turn away.

Hoskuld catches my elbow and swings me back around. "Is my bold Beauty actually being shy?" He holds up a brooch of twisting gold threads. "This would be a fine choice." He goes to pin it to the shoulder of my dress. I wrench myself free and back away. Hoskuld's eyes cloud with confusion. But he doesn't press me further.

"Come take care of these," he calls to a woman *þræll*. "Separate out the jewelry."

She carefully wraps the treasures in softened leather, packing the jewelry back in the casket and everything else away in a barrel.

Hoskuld puts his arm around my waist. "Your dress

is bloody from that Irish whore. I heard how she hit you. And then you went right on and helped take care of the injured. You surprise me. You're a strong one. A worthy one." He looks down at me with pride in the set of his jaw.

I want not to care. But it feels so strange to be praised, so strange and good, even if the words are Hoskuld's.

"Don't you worry about her." Hoskuld brushes his lips over my ear. "I'll sell her to the biggest lout in Iceland. She'll pay for what she did to you."

The poor Irish woman. I look toward the mast. She's still tied there. And a man stands beside her, talking. He's a priest! My hand reaches toward him involuntarily.

"Surprised, are you?" Hoskuld pulls back and smiles. "Ransom for holy men is the highest. I hope this cleric is an important one, my Beauty, my worthy *þræll*."

I walk away from him and stand at port side, staring at the distant coast of Eire. My mind plays over the brooch I refused. That's how this all began—with my looking at a brooch in a silversmith's while my poor brother Nuada became a Viking's victim. A circle closes around me, locking me in place. I feel like I cannot move. What's happening to me?

I'm so tired. It's as though I haven't slept *ó Samhain co Imbolc*—from the beginning of fall to the beginning of spring. I hold on to the rail for support.

We sail the rest of the day and I nap on and off. At one point I wake to see Torild kneeling over my patient. She unwinds his bandage. I go kneel beside her.

"You do it," says the sick man in a feeble whisper. He flicks a finger toward me. "Please. You."

Torild pays him no attention. She leans over his wound and sniffs loudly.

"You," manages the sick man. "You promised." A tear rolls down the crease across his temple into his hair.

I don't understand anything that's happening.

"Onion," declares Torild. "The wound stinks of onion. His bowels are perforated."

The man stares at me with the bluest eyes. I take his hand. If Torild is going to sew his bowels, I'll help.

Torild turns her head to Hoskuld, who's been watching from the side, along with several other free men. Hoskuld comes over and goes down on one knee beside her. "A wound like this poisons from within," says Torild.

"Ragnar is a good man, a good companion," says Hoskuld.

The man called Ragnar squeezes my hand.

"He will suffer unrelenting pain," says Torild.

Hoskuld drops his head. His chin falls on his chest. His eyes close.

"His screams will shake the faith of everyone who hears them," says Torild. "And then he will die anyway."

Hoskuld stands and walks to his companions. They move as a unit to the other side of the deck.

Torild takes out a pair of gold earrings from a chest. She slaps my hand away from Ragnar's with a *tsk*. She puts the earrings on him and bows her head. "Accept this payment for his entrance to the afterlife," she mutters. "Please."

"Please," echoes Ragnar, but those eyes are on me, blue ice in his sweaty face.

Two *þrælar* lift him with one swift motion and swing him over the side. I clap my hand over my mouth to hold in the scream.

That's what he meant.

Now he's gone, drowned at sea.

And after I promised.

How many people have I failed? This will be the last time, I swear to myself.

CHAPTER TWENTY-ONE:
RANSOM

The sails are lowered and all three ships are tied together again. We're near a small, rocky beach. It's late afternoon. The raven cage is uncovered, so I know we're not raiding. The birds screamed for a while, then finally calmed down.

The three *þrælar* closest to me talk in hushed tones. They disagree over what the burial of my patient would have been like if we'd been back in the north country.

"He would have been placed in the stern of a boat loaded with food, drink, his horse, his dog, his most prized possessions." The man looks around, then whispers, "Even a *þræll* or two. The ship would have been set afire and let loose to sail down a river out to sea."

"Never," says another. "He wasn't rich and important enough for that."

"Right," says a third. "If he was that rich, he'd never have agreed to go to such an isolated and distant settlement as Iceland."

"Hoskuld is going to Iceland," says the first, "and he's

both rich and important." He rubs his chest in satisfaction at his argument.

The other two go quiet and look distant for a moment.

"Well, he wouldn't be burned, anyway," says the second man finally. "He'd have been buried in blue clay, covered with stones."

"And perhaps," adds the third man, "perhaps inside that grave he'd be in a small boat with some jewelry."

I'm fascinated. The rites of these people are so strange. And I'm surprised that a burial at sea should be so different from their normal burials. But this wasn't a burial: Ragnar wasn't dead yet; he was disposed of, as though he didn't exist. Hoskuld was trying to protect morale, but how can a secret do that when everyone knows it and everyone pretends not to?

Out of the corner of my eye, I see Hoskuld and his companions—the other free men on this journey—gathering at the prow of our ship. Something's about to happen.

I leave the *þrælar* and move as close to those men as I can without making it obvious that I'm eavesdropping.

The priest's hands are tied behind his back. I learn they're going to exchange him for the ransom on this isolated beach. Apparently a Viking arranged this with another priest, who is to bring lots of silver. All this negotiation in the middle of a raid.

Two weeks ago I would have shaken my head in dis-belief at such action. But I know a little bit about Hoskuld by this point. If I assume all Vikings are like Hoskuld, then I can understand what this other man did now. Vikings may act like they've lost their minds, but it's false. They've always got an eye on business, even when they're attacking like maniacs.

"Take me, too," screams the Irish woman. She's still in the sheep pit, tied to the mast, but she's standing tall and her voice is strong. "I'm rich. I'm the niece of a king. I'm worth a ransom." She can't have heard what they're say-ing from where she is. And she doesn't understand Norse anyway, I'm sure. But she's figured out what's going on.

She's smart.

Hoskuld looks at her. Does he understand Gaelic? He walks over and questions her in Norse.

"You stupid Viking!" screams the woman. "Don't you even know the Gaelic word for ransom? What about *rí tuaithe*—tribal king—do you know that? What words do you know? *Dán*—gift—you idiot. My father will give you a gift for me. *Dán dán dán.*"

Hoskuld hits her in the side of the head so hard, I wonder if she'll go deaf. I jerk back and choke in a yelp.

"Don't you go feeling pity again," he says, looking at me. "She's a vixen. Vicious."

He didn't understand her words. He doesn't speak Gaelic. But he understood her tone. He knew he was being insulted. Maybe she's not that smart.

Hoskuld climbs out of the sheep pit and produces a thin rope. "I'm going ashore again." He comes at me, then he stops, and with his eyes fastened on mine, he drops the rope. "You can do more good with your hands free, Beauty. Besides, you'll be under watchful eyes." He jerks his head toward a man who's clearly standing guard. "I won't be long." He leaves me with a kiss.

Hoskuld and a group of three companions take up swords and shields. They disappear on the shore with the hostage priest. While they're gone, a man tells stories— this time about Thor. But I'm too sleepy to listen. I sink to my haunches and doze off.

✦　✦　✦

"Sister." The word is in Gaelic. I open my eyes to see a young man jump into the sheep pit. At first I'm so groggy from sleep, I think he's talking to me. My Nuada. But then I see he has two hands.

I stand and look around. The ships are sailing under first moonlight. I slept a long time.

The Irish woman stares at the new man. "Findan!

You didn't let them take you captive, did you?"

"They're no better than savages. Father heard the priest was being ransomed here, so he sent me with a ransom for you. Instead, they took the money and me."

"Is every man on Earth a complete dunce?" The Irish woman curses, with words that I've never heard from a woman's mouth before. "Rabbit eaters. You let rabbit eaters catch you."

"So did you," says the man, Findan. But he sounds more frustrated than angry.

We Irish don't eat rabbit. But, like this woman, I've heard that Vikings do, though I haven't seen it yet.

Findan puts his head in his hands and sways on his feet. For a moment I think he'll fall under the sheep and get stepped on. Instead he climbs out of the pit and sits on the deck not far from me.

I wonder why his hands aren't tied. Does Hoskuld think he's such a fool he wouldn't have the sense to try to escape? The man sighs loudly. I think he's crying. Maybe Hoskuld is right that he's worthless.

Young þrælar hand out dinner. One of them gives me a slab of beef jerky and an apple. It's late to be eating, and I find I'm ravenous. I seek out a second apple and eat it, core and all. I chew on the meat like a wild thing, and energy comes. I find I'm actually jumpy.

Hoskuld squats in a circle with his companions. They're arguing. I wander closer.

"It was wrong to take that Irish man—that Findan— when he came only to bargain. We'll regret it."

"That's true. If word gets around, everyone will be afraid we Vikings won't keep our part of deals. No one will pay us ransoms anymore."

Hoskuld pounds his fist on the deck. Capturing Findan was his idea, clearly. "That Findan has no brains. Who will care if he's gone?" But, despite his fist-banging, his objection lacks force. He knows he's made a mistake. And the others know he knows it. They're quiet for a moment.

Finally someone says, "Findan must be released. Where's the best place to dump him?"

"And not just him," chimes in someone else, "the woman, too. She'll never be of use to anyone."

"Tir Chonaill. It's not far. We can get rid of the two of them easy. I'll take care of everything."

I go back to sitting on the deck near the Irish man. Findan. I watch his sister. I won't fall asleep now. I will fend off the weariness that waits beside me like a hungry dog.

"Pull in near those rocks," someone says. It's darker now. It must be close to midnight.

"Can you swim?" one of Hoskuld's companions asks Findan. He's the one who said he'd take care of everything.

Findan doesn't answer.

"Irish don't swim any better than Norse do," says another man. "We have to set them on the shore."

All three ships lower their sail. Then ours rows ahead. I stand up so I can see. That's my home out there, my Eire. Yet I have no plan. I feel suspended in time.

And now we're beside the rock. The ravens set up their clamor anew.

"Get off," shouts the man who spoke to Findan before.

"Not without my sister," shouts back Findan, in passable Norse.

"She's coming. And good riddance to her."

I watch as another man jumps into the sheep pit to untie the woman.

Hoskuld comes to stand beside me. He puts an arm around my waist and says in my ear, "You're worth ten Irish women, even royalty like her."

I look into his eyes. Hoskuld is the most powerful chieftain of Iceland—he could change the whole way people do things in the new settlement, the whole way they think about slavery. If he wanted to. He turns his back and looks out over the water. But I keep my eye on Findan's sister.

The woman is free. She races through the sheep, leaps onto the deck, and rams right into me. Again! Head first, smack in the middle of my chest. I'm flat on my back, breathless.

Hoskuld swirls around. "You vile vixen!" He picks up the Irish woman from behind.

"Did you think I didn't see you?" she screams at me in Gaelic, kicking and thrashing. "You and your sneaky eyes. You were up to something. Well, you can't hurt us now, filthy pig." And Hoskuld hurls her over the side.

I lie here looking up at stars, amazed at everything. And I sob, silently.

What are all these tears about? I cried after we stole those children. Cried and cried. I'm on the verge of crying all the time these days. And I hate crying. I have no respect for adults who cry. I'm stronger than that. I'm the one who helped Torild.

But of course I'm crying. The sail is up. We're moving fast. Away from Eire. And I did nothing to escape. I didn't see an opportunity, it's true. But the fact is, I'm not sure I would have taken one. I'm not sure where I belong. I don't know anything for sure anymore. All I know is that I'm sad to put Eire behind forever. I cry for all that will never be.

My chest aches so.

Hoskuld throws a blanket over me and crawls in under. He holds me close. "Hush now. She's gone. I had to let her leave alive, for the sake of our reputations. Besides, I know you wouldn't have wanted me to kill her. But she'll never hurt you again. No one will ever hurt you again, Beauty. You are mine. My joy."

He couldn't be more wrong. I am no one's.

CHAPTER TWENTY-TWO:
BRID

I don't know what wakes me. It isn't morning yet. Everyone is asleep except the men watching the sails.

There. A flapping noise. Not the flap of a sail. The sails are tight and full. And their flap is loud anyway. This is something small.

I ease out from under Hoskuld's heavy arm and sit up, pulling the edge of the blanket to my chin. The moon is bright tonight. It glows off the blond and red hair of the sleepers. It plays on the pinkish skin of the almost bald sheep.

What is that noise?

A bird bounces from the back of one sheep to another. A bird. What's it doing out here, in the middle of the sea?

I get up and pad quietly to the edge of the sheep pit.

The bird pecks at the back of the sheep. It's eating. Frantically. It's eating like something that has been starving. Like me, when I had those apples last night.

I look out over the ship sides. To the aft the outline

of land still shows. But on all other sides, there's just sea. A person could never swim that distance, but for the bird it's manageable. The bird should head back to land now, before we get too far.

I rub my hands together lightly and rapidly, giving off a sound loud enough for a bird's ears, but too soft to wake a person.

It swivels its head to face me, eyes forward. It's about double the size of a pigeon, and its head is decidedly pigeonlike. But those eyes leave no room for confusion: This is a bird of prey.

There's no potential prey for a bird like that on this ship. I look at the raven cage. The three black birds ignore this visitor. I'm surprised at that, too.

I lower myself gingerly into the sheep pit and push aside the stinking, sleeping bodies to get closer.

The bird watches me and jumps to the back of a sheep farther away. It really must be very hungry, to let me get this close without flying off.

I move both arms in a sudden, abrupt sweep through the air over my head.

The bird hops away one more sheep.

From so close I got a good view of its feet. Talons. Five on each foot. Like scaly hands. Powerful. This is not a sea bird. It belongs in a forest, high in the tree canopy.

This bird is in danger out here. And I bet it doesn't even drink salt water. So what will it drink? How often do birds need to drink?

I'm not sure how long I stand there motionless, but the sky grows gray with the slightest tinge of pink. I like being here amid the hot bodies of sheep. I like the roll of the sea. It induces a trancelike state.

A sheep makes droppings in her sleep. I didn't know animals could defecate asleep.

The bird jumps quickly to the floor and pecks around in the dung. It eats. I wrinkle my nose in distaste. But then I see it crack something in the side of that curved, pointed beak. Dung beetles, of course. Somehow that seems much more acceptable than eating the dung itself.

The bird eats and eats and eats. Then it hops over to the long trough of dirty water that the sheep drink from and slakes its thirst.

This bird knows the ship. I'm sure of it. It acts totally familiar with everything.

But then, what do I know about how a bird acts when it's in an unfamiliar place? I don't really know anything about animals other than the most obvious things that everyone knows.

Brigid could tell me what kind of bird this is. Brigid

followed Father's falconer around when she was smaller. Her incessant questions gave her an education about all kinds of living creatures.

Lord, how I miss my sister.

Voices. People are waking with the sun.

The bird flies in alarm. It circles slowly in the air above the ship. Its tail is long with broad brown and white bands. No, the last band at the tip is so dark, it must be black. The plumage is deep brown, lighter on the tummy. The wings are slender. Looking at it from below, it seems small and vulnerable. Nothing like those hawks that swoop down on the rats in the Downpatrick fort. This is a delicate bird. A beautiful bird.

And one I recognize. Yes, I remember now. I remember the brown bird that chased away a seagull back before this journey began. This couldn't be the same one. That doesn't make sense. Yet I feel almost certain it is. My brave companion. How delightful!

In a flash of brown and white, the bird dips in front of the ship. Out of sight now.

I climb from the sheep pit onto the front deck and look ahead for the bird. But it's gone. Disappeared. The only thing in sight is the first ship. And these ships are narrow. Plus the sea is placid—so the bird isn't hidden by waves. I have a clear view.

Did it change direction without me seeing? I turn in a circle, looking everywhere.

The bird has simply vanished.

How could that be?

An irrational sense of loss weakens me. I'm a fool. This is probably not the same bird I saw back in the north country. And even if it is, I didn't know it was here until just now. I have no right to think of it as a companion—I have not just lost a companion.

I remember the Saxon youths the night Brigid disappeared. They said, "Brid,"—bird. The word is Brigid's name with a small chunk taken out of the middle.

A wash of sadness slackens my cheeks.

Wherever you've gone, Brid, be safe. Don't be swallowed by the water. Live.

CHAPTER TWENTY-THREE:
SIGHTINGS

"Storm!" It's Asgör who makes the sighting. I've been learning the names of some of the free men now, for their names are always bandied about: Asgör, Snorri, Thorgrid, Ingvar, Göte.

I look where he points. It's easy to see it coming from far away. Black clouds on the horizon. They grow big fast.

It's going to be a powerful one, I know, because suddenly everyone rushes around tying down the chests and barrels and anything that moves. We even spread out a fishing net over the sheep and cow and tack it down at the corners. These nets are strong, made of waxed walrus-hide rope. Ingvar assures me they can hold a tremendous weight without breaking.

The clouds race toward us. The wind picks up. It's gale force in no time. My hair band goes whipping away.

The sails come down on all three ships. And now the men are tying the children by a rope around their waists to hooks on the ship sides between the oarlocks. The oars are pulled in and strapped together and battened down.

The women put on shoulder brooches. The men put on gold earrings. Adorning themselves, like Torild did the sick man before they threw him overboard. Oh, Lord. Gold chains and bracelets from the monastery casket are passed around, until everyone's wearing something. Even me—I allowed Torild to lock a bracelet on me because it seemed to matter to her so much. I allowed it, though my heart went crazy as the clasp snapped shut.

Hoskuld calls all the adults on our ship together. Everyone who isn't tied down comes to the center of the forward or aft deck and huddles tight, arms around one another. Hoskuld leads us in prayers. Every face is turned to him, hanging on his words. When going into battle, all men may be consulted, but in this moment, there is only one chief; Hoskuld is like a father to us all.

"Odin, Father of the Gods, hear us," he calls.

Everyone repeats his words exactly.

"Help us prevail on your son, Thor."

And they repeat again.

"And Thor, great god of thunder, we see your glory. When we are in Iceland, when we are farming, we will worship you for rain so plentiful as this. We will thank you for this generosity. But at sea that generosity isn't needed. Please, Thor, hear us. And Odin, great father, if we drown, please, Odin, send down the Valkyriers to take us to Valhalla, so we can feast and drink for all eternity."

Everyone repeats everything Hoskuld says.

Black blocks out the sun in an instant—as though we've entered a dark tent and dropped the flap.

And then it's here. Loud and thrashing. Waves break over the ship. We're tossed side to side for so long. Lightning flashes and thunder claps immediately after.

I hold tight to the *þræll* beside me, but a wave catches him wrong. He's swept off his feet. I make my fingers like iron, grip as hard as I can. But his arm slips out of mine, out of the man's on his other side. And he's gone, washed away in a scream of terror.

Did I scream too?

The sheep are crying. I look. It's hard to see because the raindrops come down fast and big as pebbles. The sheep whimper, like babies. I pull away from the huddle and crawl to the edge of the animal pit. So much water has come in that the sheep are knee-deep in it. Can the ship withstand the weight of all that extra water? Will it burst apart or merely sink?

I manage to stagger to one of the big wooden buckets we use for bailing and I lower myself into the pit and bail water.

Hoskuld and a handful of other men join me. We bail and bail, but we're losing the battle.

Now most of the able-bodied people are dumping the contents of barrels and boxes, and bailing too.

The shriek of the wind deafens me. I'm inside my silent head now, alone with my terror. Nothing exists but the bucket in my hands and the water I keep filling it with. Bail, bail, bail. My arms ache so badly, but I cannot stop. Bail, bail, bail. Endlessly.

Till I realize we are gaining on it. The waves are less ferocious. No more water is coming in. The wind no longer beats us. Everything is slowing down. The rain slowly peters out. And I'm falling.

✦ ✦ ✦

When I open my eyes, we're sailing again. It's late morning. The sun gleams through crystal-clear air. I slept all through the night. From the roll of the ship, I know the sea is calm again, beautifully calm.

Hoskuld sits up beside me. On seeing that I'm awake, he leans over and briefly touches his nose to mine. "You saw the sheep would drown. You bailed first. I'm lucky to own you." His lips move toward mine, then he stops. "Give a kiss, won't you? Don't make me always steal." His voice is light, almost teasing, but the small opening of his lips and the slight tilt to his head give him away. Something humbles him. I blink and regard him, unmoving.

I'm saved by the intrusion of the world around us: A woman stumbles about crying loudly. A *þræll*. The man she loved was lost in the storm. They weren't married; *þrælar* have no legal standing, so they can't marry—they can't buy or sell or inherit or anything. But she loved him. And he fathered her children. She says all this to anyone who cares to listen, and she cries.

When she reaches us, Hoskuld puts his arms around her. I pull myself up to sitting and stare. His face is sad; he's sincere. And she isn't even his *þræll*. She belongs to Ingvar.

Moaning comes from all sides. Other men went overboard too. Two free men, and two other men *þrælar*. And one woman *þræll*. And a child *þræll* was flung about so roughly that, even though he was tied to the ship, he died of his bruises. His broken body tears my heart. Women cry for the lost and the dead. I listen and watch, and I cry too.

The three ships lost seven people, in all. And two sheep. They probably died of fear. And who knows how much silver and how many tools went into the deep. Hoskuld assesses his belongings and adds his own lament, for the loss of his carpenter's tool chest especially.

It would have helped in repairing the ships. The storm took a wicked toll.

But at least the sun is trying to make up with us now. Before long everyone is talking more optimistically. They're saying the ones who went over the side have incurred no shame, for they didn't die in a cowardly way or by their own sword. They died well. These words seem to console them.

I understand honor. But to me their words are inane. There is nothing either honorable or dishonorable about being swept away at sea. It is just sad. Terribly, terribly sad.

In a flash they become all business now, all working together, free men and *þrælar*, side by side.

I should help too. There's so much to do. I reach a hand to the top edge of the ship side and pull myself to my feet. My legs are weak. And, oh! Without warning my stomach empties over the side into the sea. My forehead breaks out in sweat.

Torild is beside me with a horn of mead. I use it to wash my mouth out. I turn to nod thanks, but she's gone, tending to those battered in the storm. I feel woozy. I look out over the water again. My hair band disappeared in the storm and my stringy hair falls in my face. I knot it at the nape of my neck.

A spray shoots up not a body's length away from me. It's a narwhal. It surfaces with its tusk pointed straight to the glorious sky. It expels the air from its lungs in great spouts.

Men with those double-pronged spears have come to the ship side. They hold them at the ready. A whale would come a long way toward making us feel better about that storm.

Then a much smaller whale surfaces beside this first one. It's a cow and her calf. They must have gotten separated from the rest of the pod in the storm. And now I don't want them to kill her.

I look around for Hoskuld. But the free men are already talking it over.

Snorri says, "If we kill the mother, the calf will surely die."

Ingvar says, "If we kill the calf, the mother will grieve, and some say whales can die of grief."

"Either way," says Asgör, "it's bad policy."

They let the whales go by.

For the first time I am grateful to Vikings. Whatever the reasons for it, it was the right decision.

Three women are cutting the skins off the two dead sheep and preparing the meat. I join them, watching carefully to make sure I do this chore the way they think is right. I want to fit in. I want to be one of them, even if it's just for a moment.

The rest of the people are cleaning up the mess left by the storm. Women mend ripped tunics and cloaks. Men repair broken oars. Children gather things that have been tossed helter-skelter.

We eat our fill of mutton stew. The *þræll* called Deirdre complains that we have no way to salt the rest of it. Our barrel of salt was swept overboard in the storm. We have to soak the rest in seawater in one of the bailing barrels that used to hold who knows what.

The day goes on in slow, deliberate work. The people pull together, letting go of their grief. Either these are callous folk or they know a bottomless well of courage.

That evening the storytelling goes on longer than usual. Snorri has the honor tonight, and he's one of the best, so everyone comes close. I understand almost every word—about brave men slaying dragons and roasting their hearts.

When it ends, Hoskuld says, "Listen, everyone. Listen hard." He cups a hand behind his ear and stretches that ear toward the sky. "Can you hear it?"

Everyone mimics him.

"I hear nothing," says Ingvar.

"Exactly." Hoskuld looks around at us solemnly.

"That's the sound of Thor sleeping. There will be no thunder tonight. Odin has encouraged his son to rest." Hoskuld lifts his chin. "We thank you, powerful Odin," he calls loudly. "Thank you for this rest."

Everyone repeats his words exactly.

Hoskuld looks around at us again. "There will be much frolicking in Valhalla tonight, for my lost companions took every single *þræll* whisked away by the storm with them, even the woman and child. So all of us can be placid tonight, like the sea, like Thor. Sleep in peace."

Everyone repeats, "Sleep in peace." They wander off and nestle together in little sleeping groups.

Hoskuld takes my hand and pulls me down on the deck with him, near the rear mast. He curls on his side and sleeps. Our blanket was among the losses of the storm, so he's wrapped himself in a cloak, like everyone else. I'm glad for the loss of blankets. It means we cannot wrap the raven cage to make us silent for a raid.

I sit beside Hoskuld with an odd sense of contentment. He's been a good chieftain through this crisis, and the way he put us all to sleep tonight felt like a benevolent father. I remember his request this morning, his plea for a kiss. I lean and brush my lips softly over his cheek. He gives a small moan that makes me straighten up quickly. I look around.

There is only one man tending the rudder tonight; it's Göte. Everyone else is too exhausted, and the sea is soft, anyway, so one is enough. Göte sees me look at him, and he nods. It's a tiny thing—a simple nod. But it feels so familiar, like he knows me, like he's acknowledging that the shared misery of the storm has bound us together. My hand rises of its own accord in a small, responding wave. But Göte has already turned his face to the stars for direction.

That's when it happens: I see the bird again. At first I think it's a vision. The spirit of Brigid, come to bring me a message. But Göte calls out to me, "Look." His voice is astonished. "Look, a honey buzzard. A female." So I know she's real. And now I know what kind of bird she is. A honey buzzard. I'm so happy to know that, I'm so thankful to Göte, this man who nods and knows the names of birds, this Viking.

The bird goes sheep-hopping, of course. I could laugh, she's such a pleasure to watch. But it looks like the pickings are slim. The storm must have washed away insects. It washed away dung heaps, too. And the trough holds nothing but seawater. We had little enough fresh water as it was—only enough for the smallest children and the animals. But that barrel got knocked over in the storm.

Alas, poor Brid. My throat hurts for her. The crazy thing is doomed.

CHAPTER TWENTY-FOUR:
A BRIEF LAYOVER

Nothing about this new land we're approaching looks welcoming. The sky is overcast. The coastline is fogged in. The winds are high. The air is cool and wet, even at midday. It sits on my cheeks like a dead thing. The place is a cluster of so many islands and they all look rugged and rocky. I see no forests. Nothing that makes these Faeroe Islands appear inhabitable. Torild says this will be our last stop before the final long sea days to Iceland.

We skirt past the coastal cliffs and steer toward one of the larger islands. As we row into a harbor sheltered by a smaller island, Deirdre and Torild and Gunnhild talk beside me in happy tones. I know the names of all the women *prælar* on my ship now, of course. They've wrapped themselves up tight in their cloaks and are shivering in the fog just as hard as anyone, so I don't understand their excitement. They seem as foolish as the ravens, who set up their customary cawing as we neared land.

Asgör is the first to see. Again. Even though he's grayhaired, he must have the best eyes. He shouts and points.

I can just make out a town near the shore. The people are turning out to greet us. They're cheering. In Norse.

We disembark, stumbling on dry ground as though we're drunk. I didn't know we were getting off. I'm grateful for this respite from the sea but worried at the prospect of staying in such a dismal place.

The people from all three ships are led into a giant town hall. Women and *þrælar* spring into action, while men talk and drink beer. The island *þrælar* are mostly dark-haired, with hooked noses and red cheeks. I wonder if they were all stolen from the same place. The traditional description of the legendary Finn comes to mind: hair like a raven, cheeks like blood, body like snow. But the Irish say this with appreciation; they find Finn handsome. I bet none of the free people here finds these *þrælar* handsome. They treat them roughly, shouting orders and pushing them about.

We cook the rest of the mutton from the sheep that died in the storm. The townsfolk contribute roast pig and goat as well. I go with one of the women to dig up a barrel of butter, buried in the earth to keep it from going rancid. We bring it inside and make hot cakes for dessert. The children from our ships play with the town children. They kick balls off the walls and no one shouts at them to go outside; they'd get lost in the fog, after all.

By evening it's one enormous party with singing, dancing, storytelling. One man plays a harp of carved willow wood that looks so much like a harp Father's manservant played that I gasp.

All my old curiosity about what happens in these halls is finally satisfied. It's like an Irish party, just louder, drunker, rowdier. And just as infectious; I find myself moving in time to the music.

News of Torild's skills at healing has gotten around. A woman pulls her by the hand through the hall. But first Torild grabs me with her other hand. She tells everyone I'm her assistant. I feel strangely flattered. Torild lances boils, administers angelica for ailing digestive systems, smears herbal ointments on skin disorders, and I mimic her as exactly as I can. People thank us profusely.

The evening wears on, and some of the men stagger outdoors in a sodden stupor. Other men and women pair off and disappear.

Hoskuld finds me and drags me to a corner. We haven't talked since he asked me to give him a kiss of my own accord. He's drunk now, and he lavishes kisses on me just as he used to—without a hint of hesitation. "You're better than I ever dreamed a woman could be," he says, slurring his words. "You can do anything. Anything and everything." His eyes are full of wonder. At me. And though he's far from lucid, I can't help but repeat his words in my head.

I close my eyes, and he does what he wants. The music and drink plus the healing work with Torild have combined to make me mellow. And Hoskuld's praise lingers. There is no pain tonight, for the first time. I feel nothing but gentle warmth.

Hoskuld falls asleep at last. I'm tired too. And dizzy. I drift off slowly into water-logged dreams.

The women wake first. We drank less than the men, after all. I go outside to an outhouse. Men sleep here and there, wherever they dropped last night. I wander past them all, down to the harbor. The three ships rock slowly on a sea that looks harmless.

A bird flies from somewhere inland out to the boats. It circles overhead. It's the honey buzzard. My honey buzzard. I'm sure of it. My clasped hands press under my chin in joy. I have to remind myself this bird is real, not Brigid in disguise. But she moves me just as strongly as if she were. And what harm is there in feeling sisterly toward her? In some sense, I'm still *aist* myself—we are both birds.

She disappears into the dragon's mouth carved on the prow of my ship. Ah!

There's no one about at the harbor. I strip down to

my smallclothes and wade out to the ship. I climb aboard with the help of a rope. Then I walk along the wide ledge on the top of the side. I'm high above the water level. A wave of nausea hits me. I swallow over and over and concentrate on being still, inside and out. It eases off and I risk moving again.

When the side curves up toward the dragon head, I have to stop. I hug the edge and peer up. From this angle all I can see is the very edge of the mouth: Stray twigs lie there. I knew it. I'm grinning. I knew.

The honey buzzard peeks out at me just at that moment. Her vulnerability opens like an offering. I respond with equal vulnerability; I whisper, "Your *rún*—secret—is safe with me, Brid. We both have secrets." I'm astonished to hear my voice, even muted like this. Oh, Lord, how I miss talking. For an instant I feel as though I've risen from the dead, as though I'm the me who had a family, who whispered to a sister.

On a sudden whim, I let go and fall backward into the water. It's shallow, but not so shallow that I hurt myself. I swim all around the ship. I'm happy. I'm happy that Brid isn't crazy.

Or maybe she is. Clearly she made that nest when the boat was on land, back before we started this journey. That's why she chased away the seagull. She was protecting her nest. When the ships set sail, though, she should have deserted her eggs and flown back to the life she knew.

But here she is. She's suffered hunger and thirst. She's been battered by a storm. And now we're at an island where she could stay in the blessèd trees and be safe. But she's back on her nest.

She's a fine parent. As good a parent as a stork.

I'm deliriously happy. I swim and swim and swim, until I'm so tired, all I can do is float.

A shout comes from the shore. A woman stands there waving to me, calling me in. I get out and pull my dress on over my dripping smallclothes.

I follow the woman back to the town hall. We spend the morning refilling barrels with fresh water and loading up on vegetables and dried meats, since so much of our larder was lost in the storm. I work as hard as anyone, merging with the group of women.

Hoskuld gives the villagers sheep and some of our remaining silver, and takes, in return, several goats and a pregnant sow.

Everyone hugs, and the women give us bundles of flatbreads. I'm particularly grateful to see them. Flatbread seems to be the only food that makes me feel good these days. They calm my queasy stomach. I'm getting sicker, it's clear. I don't have fever or chills. But my energy lags. Swimming around the ship this morning just about undid me.

Before we get on the ship, a woman with a child clinging to her skirts gives me a small pouch. "These are just for you," she says. Surprised, I go to open it, but her hand stays mine. "Wait till the others are asleep." I hug her especially hard. Then I climb aboard with everyone else.

Except Göte. He stands on the shore.

"Come along," calls Hoskuld. "Hurry."

"I'm staying here," calls back Göte.

"Weren't you the one who complained about hunger back on Brännö Island?" Hoskuld's voice cajoles, but there's a threat behind it. "The life of a free man in Iceland can be very good, indeed. Didn't you beg me to let you come work so you could earn enough to buy your own land, have your own homestead?"

It's true; I remember. Göte begged fervently.

"After that storm, well . . . ," calls Göte, shaking his head. "I hate the open seas now."

Hoskuld's eyes flash anger. His hands close into fists.

I grab Hoskuld's arm, to stop him from jumping out and bashing the man in the name of morale, as he did the *þræll* who talked of fearing the sea early in our journey—the *þræll* whose name I now know is Hlif.

Hoskuld looks at me with an open mouth, ready to protest. Then his eyes change. He folds his big hand over mine.

I move close to him, and we watch as the townspeople take Göte in gladly. I imagine this is the only way they ever get anyone new to come live in this dismal land. I will miss Göte. He's the one who nodded to me the night we both saw Brid. He's the one who told me Brid is a honey buzzard.

We set out, our bellies full from the midday meal. I wave to the women on shore. They've set fires and boil seawater to get salt, because they gave us most of their own supply. They wave back. I wonder if they're wistful.

I wish we could take them with us. All of them. I'd like to rescue them from these dank islands. They should be nothing to me. But I feel I know them. They are generous and warm.

I wave and wave.

CHAPTER TWENTY-FIVE: TRUST

We travel over open sea at great speed. The waves come like sliding mountains, miraculous green towers on the starboard aft quarter. A strong wind blows from the northeast. We hang on, but we aren't afraid. Rather, it's exhilarating. Viking ships are made for exactly this. Our ship moves so smoothly through the changing water that at times it seems as if we're on a large living animal, instead of a collection of wood.

The horizon where the sky meets the sea is only a couple of hundred yards in every direction. I feel like no matter what we do, where we turn, we're heading off into an abyss. But I don't care. This moment is good.

Last night, after Hoskuld fell asleep, I opened the pouch that the island woman gave me. It was full of boiled seagull eggs. There is nothing particularly wonderful about seagull eggs. Yet I found myself ravenous for them. And they worked wonders, making my two otherwise constant companions, exhaustion and nausea, leave for a while. I ate them all, as I watched Brid eating even more greedily. The bird hopped from animal to animal, obviously pleased at the variety the newcomers lent to her diet. She feasted on goat ticks and hog lice. I wished she'd eat the fleas off me. They drive me batty sometimes.

Today we've been eating the new flatbread and peas. We planned on having dried meat for our evening meal. But the memory of the feast at the island town hall two nights ago lingers, making the men hungry for fresh flesh.

So when the wind lets up a little, they cast fishnets. Older children uncoil lines and run wax along them. They attach a hook at one end and drop them into the water. We eat delicious bass and cod. There's so much, we pickle a good portion of the cod for later.

After we clean up, people gather for stories. I don't care to listen tonight, though. I go to the aft, near Snorri, who's working the rudder. Something catches my eye. I look toward the first ship, which is ahead and slightly to starboard. A man pushes another overboard. I gasp.

The man goes underwater, but he comes up again. He knows how to swim!

I grab Snorri and point.

He sets up the alarm.

The sail comes down. Someone throws a piece of driftwood tied to a rope. It lands near the man, but a wave comes between them. The man disappears underwater.

The other two boats have pulled down their sails now too. Everyone's watching.

The man surfaces. He swims for the driftwood and latches on just as another wave comes. Cheers go up.

We pull him in. As he comes over the side into our ship, he cries, "Have pity on me," and falls to his knees.

"What are you talking about?" says Hoskuld, quickly coming forward. It's clear from the man's clothes that he is a *þræll*. Yet Hoskuld wraps him in a blanket he bought from the islanders. Hoskuld is tender, sweetly tender. I wonder if he ever had a brush with drowning.

"My master threw me overboard."

Hoskuld steps back in distaste. "You must have done something awful to make him do that."

"I did. But only because he forced me. I stole a brooch for him. Then he wanted to kill me, so no one could ever tell what happened."

Hoskuld's face squinches in a frown. "Who is your master?"

"Brynjolf. Please don't send me back to him. He'll only kill me."

Brynjolf. I've heard the name before. But because he's not from our ship, I don't know him.

"Whose brooch was it originally?" asks Hoskuld.

"Egil's."

"Egil?" Hoskuld puts his hands on his hips. "He's a *goði*—a local chieftain—just like me." He takes down the horn that hangs on the mast and blows loudly to call the ships together. The sea has calmed enough to do that without risk. "Egil," calls out Hoskuld.

"Here I am, friend." A stout man comes to the side of the first ship.

"Are you missing a brooch?"

Egil goes to his chest and searches through it. "Yes," he calls back. "A fine one too."

"Brynjolf," Hoskuld calls out.

"Here I am, friend." He's the man I saw push the *þræll* overboard.

"Did you order your *þræll* to steal Egil's brooch?"

"No!"

"Did you push him overboard?"

"No!"

I grab Hoskuld's arm and shake it.

He pulls away. "Not now, Beauty." He doesn't know I was the one who first saw this *þræll* in the water. He has no idea.

I pinch his arm as hard as I can.

Hoskuld jerks his head toward me in annoyance. Then he blinks and stares at my eyes. Slowly he turns to Brynjolf. "If we searched your personal chest, are you saying we wouldn't find Egil's brooch?"

"There are a few brooches in my chest. I traded for them fairly. Like everyone else. And you have no authority to search my things. This isn't a general assembly. You can't settle a dispute. Besides, all of us lost things in the storm. If Egil's missing a brooch, probably it's at the bottom of the sea, along with many of my things."

Hoskuld rubs his mouth. "Why would your *þræll* lie?"

"He's crazy."

"Then you don't want him anymore?" asks Hoskuld.

"He should die. He's not trustworthy."

Hoskuld looks at the *þræll*. "We'll test you, to see if you're trustworthy. If you pass, I'll take you as my *þræll*."

The *þræll* vomits a whoosh of seawater. His face goes pale. He shakes. He didn't shake when we pulled him up over the side out of the cold ocean. But he's shaking now.

I understand. If he fails, he'll wind up back in the sea. Whatever this test is, it's unfair; Brynjolf lied about throwing the *þræll* overboard. I bet he lied about the brooch, too.

Someone's already reviving the fire from dinner. A vat of water is hung over it. Hoskuld looks at me sideways and raises one finger toward me, forbidding me to move.

He drops two stones into the vat. When the water boils, Hoskuld steps back. "It's time," he says to the þræll.

The þræll comes forward. He looks around at the crowd. Everyone's watching. His face crumples. His lips pull back from his teeth. He shoots his left hand into the water and shrieks as it comes out with a stone. His forearm and hand are bright red. Tears stream down his face. He's screaming and screaming.

There's still one stone left in the vat. I won't let this happen. I step toward Hoskuld, but someone grabs me hard from behind. "Don't," comes the whisper in my ear. "I'll take care of him." I look over my shoulder into Torild's face as I hear the second stone hit the deck.

Torild rushes to the þræll with a bucket of fresh seawater. Another woman is supporting the þræll, because he's collapsed, beyond screams. Torild plunges his red arm into the cold bucket. A boy stands ready with another bucket of water just drawn from the sea. After a few moments, Torild moves the þræll's arm to that bucket, while the boy goes to refill the first. Torild moves the þræll's arm five times before she's satisfied.

I watch all this closely, panting in my distress. Now she beckons me even closer. She whispers, "Lean over me from this side and spread out your cloak so people can't see what I'm doing."

I shield the *þræll*'s arm so that only Torild and I see what she does now. No one else still watching knows. But there aren't many left anyway. The sails are back up and we're moving again. People have broken into their small sleeping clusters. They're talking softly.

Torild smears an ointment on the blistering arm. She wraps it in moss and winds a white cloth bandage over arm and hand. "You were smart to use the same hand twice," she says to him. "This way you'll always have at least one usable limb. You're smart."

The whole time the *þræll*'s gaze is fixed somewhere far away, as though pain has stupefied him. His pupils are large. His breath is shallow. I take his right hand, the healthy hand, to give him comfort. It's cold and clammy. He has the tremors.

Torild pours mead down his throat. "This will help," she murmurs. She fixes her one good eye on me. "Nothing went on this arm except a clean bandage. Nothing. Those are the rules. When we remove the bandage, in two days, if the wounds are healing well, this is a trustworthy man."

Why she has taken me into her confidence, I don't know. In a world of such brutality and injustice, how does anyone dare such a thing? How can kindness survive?

The day ends, and I wait till snores come from every direction. Then I leave Hoskuld's side and lower myself into the animal pit. Brid's eating, as I knew she would be. I come within arm's reach of her and she doesn't even hesitate in her scavenging. What a smart creature. She counts on me to be a friend.

Like Torild.

I weep. What a foolish expression of gratitude. But my body acts of its own accord. How lucky am I, to have the privilege of being counted on.

CHAPTER TWENTY-SIX:
HOME

The last two days I've spent much of my time sleeping or standing near Asgör. I am tired or nauseated or both almost all the time. And this old man's voice soothes me. I listen while he tells how in spring a journey like this one amounts to simply following the black-tailed godwits and the curlews, but in late summer, like now, there are no birds going to Iceland, so it's only the wave patterns and prevailing winds that guide him. I look at the water where he points, but I don't see the messages myself. The ocean simply roils in my eyes. But I marvel at Asgör's skills, which he is clearly proud of. And I like him for the patient way he explains things to me.

It's close to midday when Hoskuld calls the people on our ship together. "Time for the proof," he announces, and everyone knows what he's talking about. We've all been expecting this since we woke today.

I rush to Torild's side, and she doesn't even fix her good eye on me. She merely touches the back of my hand in acknowledgment. We are a team now. She never has to come looking for me. When she's needed somewhere, I go as well, automatically. I'll make her glad she picked me as her assistant. I'll prove she was right to trust me. I watch her carefully now, ready to follow her lead.

Olaf—that's the *þræll*'s name—sits with his back against a chest. His eyes widen, his mouth falls open, his good hand clutches the cloth of his tunic. I remember Ragnar's face when he knew he was about to be thrown overboard. He said "please" to me, just like I am saying "please" to the Lord inside my head right now. Please, please.

We play the same game, Torild and I, with me leaning over in my wide cloak and her on the other side, so no one can see her remove not just the cloth, but the moss underneath. Then Torild and I fall back to give a clear view to everyone: Olaf's arm is raw. But there's no pus.

Hoskuld raises a fist high and declares, "This *þræll* is trustworthy." He doesn't hide the victorious pleasure in his voice. That Brynjolf is despicable. I'm glad Hoskuld got the best of him. I'm glad Olaf will live. I'm so insanely glad at everything.

"There's healing yet to do," says Torild. She holds out a wad of moss before Hoskuld's face and stares up at him. "He's your *þræll* now. What's your decision?"

Hoskuld slaps himself on the chest in triumph. "Take care of him however you think best, Torild."

And so Torild and I administer more ointment, more moss, and a clean cloth. And the whole time Olaf keeps shaking his head in happy disbelief.

As soon as the new bandage is in place, Hoskuld steps forward and shakes Olaf's healthy hand. "Congratulations, Olaf." I am the one shaking my head in happy disbelief now. Hoskuld shook the hand of a *þræll*! I'm smiling so hard, my cheeks hurt.

Hoskuld grins at me. He picks me up and swings me in a circle. When he stops, he kisses me. And I am so caught in the joy of the moment, I kiss him back. His eyes fly open with a gasp of delight.

"You were right, Beauty." He smoothes my hair away from my face with both hands and cups my cheeks lovingly. "There's no one like you, Beauty. No one in the whole world. I'll keep you with me always. You'll be my most important *þræll*. My greatest treasure."

I step back from him quickly. It's as though night has fallen in an instant. And here I thought Hoskuld had finally come to understand. I spin on my heel and race across the deck, though I've nowhere to go, no way to escape.

"Can't you ever be satisfied?" he calls after me in exasperation. And I know he's angry that others have witnessed me refusing him. But it's his fault for making a spectacle—for saying those things when people had gathered to see Olaf's arm. At least he doesn't follow me now. At least he knows better than that.

But I was wrong; Hoskuld comes stomping after me. He grabs me by an elbow and yanks me to one side of the ship, pinning me there. His mouth moves in little twitches. A muscle on his jaw jumps. And then, in an instant, his whole face crumples.

"I don't know what you want. Maybe you want everything. You want to be free, that much I know."

Yes. I fix my eyes on his firmly. Yes, Hoskuld. But not just me. Free all your slaves. Then your companions might too.

He shakes his head slowly and his eyes glisten. "You could buy your freedom if you had a way to earn money. I suppose I could let you work as a healer. Still, Beauty, if our world changed, if the order of things were undone, what would happen then?" His hands move up my arms, up my throat. They hold my head. His eyes beg. "You're marvelous. A mystery I fear I will never tire of. Do you hear me? I fear that, because you can only lead to heartache. You're unreachable." He takes a deep breath. "If I free you, I risk losing you entirely." He closes his eyes, bends down, and rests his forehead heavy against mine. "We are caught." His voice cracks with sorrow. "This is the way the world is."

Such sadness undoes me. My hands rise as though to touch his cheeks. But I am as unable to accept what is as he is to change it. I stop my hands at his chest. All my strength flows against him, pushing harder and harder. I keep my eyes down.

He finally leaves.

I force back tears. Then I look around. The *þrælar* are preparing the midday meal. I help serve. I rush about, avoiding Hoskuld, not meeting anyone's eyes.

After the meal, Asgör calls out, "Attention, everyone." Another announcement? I hug myself. "The raven has not returned!" Everyone cheers.

I hug myself harder. We will be landing in Iceland today, that's what Asgör's words mean. He let free a raven yesterday morning and it returned to the ship before midday. He let free another this morning, but today's raven hasn't returned. That means it found land. Asgör explained everything to me. I can hardly believe it. This voyage has come to seem interminable. Iceland was a mirage. But we will be there today, on the ground, with the people of the settlement. All that, perhaps before the stars come out.

Immediately almost every free man on all three ships busies himself with grooming. Head hair, facial hair, nails, teeth, everything. They put away their travel clothes, grimy after having been lived in all this time, and take out their other outfit. They don knee-length, full-skirted tunics gathered at the waist by ornately buckled belts, with a drawstring at the neck. The sleeves are long, blousy at the top and fitted from elbow to cuff. The necks are braided or embroidered. The trousers are tucked into boots. And everything is in colors. The richer the man, the brighter the colors.

Hoskuld doesn't ask for my help in his self-ministrations. Maybe he actually has the good grace to realize that since he's cleaning himself up for his wife, he shouldn't be asking his concubine to tweeze his nose hairs. If he angers her too much, she could divorce him. Viking women have that right. Snorri talks some-times about his first wife, and his second, and his third. Everyone divorces him, that's what he said to me.

I smiled then. Snorri's simple manner disarms me. He's a sweet man, really. I don't condone divorce, of course. But I can't say with all certainty that I wouldn't do it if Hoskuld were my husband and he brought home a concubine.

My face must have softened just now as I was think-ing of Snorri, for Hoskuld approaches me, if somewhat gingerly. "Come look in my personal chest, Beauty. Choose a dress. Any dress." I look him straight in the face and stare coldly. He gives an exasperated sigh and leaves again.

But I am right to make this choice. All the women on this voyage are going about their normal duties. They are *þrælar*, so they don't have other clothes to put on. I refuse to be the exception. I choose the dress I've worn all journey long, even though this fine blue linen smells more of my sickness than of the sea now.

It's better that I enter this new life disheveled, anyway. I expect to be hated by everyone in Hoskuld's household. If I come in looking all fresh and fancy, as though I'm a real challenge to his wife, they'll hate me even more.

People talk about what's ahead now. Some are returning home, but a few free men and many of the *þrælar* have never been there before. So the ones who know the place describe it. Volcanoes. Glaciers. Hardly any wildlife. Not many trees, and those that grow there are stunted.

But wonderful waterfalls that cascade down cliffs. And fjords just as beautiful as back in the north country. And small horses that run wild. And plenty of birds in summer.

Are there honey buzzards? Brid will need company.

Are there storks? Huge, marvelous musterings like in Eire in spring and summer?

I listen closely, hoping someone will list all the birds that come to Iceland. But no one does.

As the sun goes down, Torild brings me a basin of fresh water and a pinch of salt. "Clean your face and teeth at least. All that vomit has left its traces."

I tilt my head at her. Why should she care? I'm a useful assistant no matter what I look like.

She draws a flatbread out of her bodice and gives it to me. I'd thought they were all gone. I smile; she's pulled this trick before. But then I look into her eyes and I realize she knows I'm sick. Of course. That lazy eye is deceptive. Torild watches everyone. She knows everything that's going on. If there were a cure for me, she'd have offered it by now. Am I dying? Nausea comes every day worse than the last. I am failing quickly.

"Take this bread," says Torild. "And tomorrow, when we land, you can have all the flatbread you want. The nausea won't last forever. Just a couple more months. What will you name him?"

I stare at her, bewildered.

She laughs. "Okay. Don't talk. But you'll talk to him, I wager." She puts the flatbread on my lap and leaves.

What will I name him?

And I suddenly know. I haven't had my monthly blood since before Hoskuld bought me. Almost two months now. I thought that was because of the illness. But I'm not dying. I'm alive.

And I'm not alone. We are together. I put my hands on my flat belly. *Immalle.*

Hoskuld's child lives within me. A tingling sensation runs through my body. That stranger I so abhorred at first, a part of him has found purchase in me. I should want to turn myself inside out. But I don't. I don't hate Hoskuld anymore. I know him too well now. I move my hands in a circle.

Lord, there are so many beautiful names, so many names that would suit a beautiful baby.

And Torild is right. I'll talk to this child. I'll chatter away. I'll sing loud and long in the language that is my birthright. And I'll tell stories. That's what I have to do. That's exactly what I have to do. That's this child's legacy. I may never see Eire again. How could I? It is weeks away by sea. But I can hold on to Eire in stories, and I can give my baby Irish heritage in tales of Finn and Cúchulainn and the warrior queen Medb and all the others. I can find them in my memory. Already I can hear Nuada telling tales. I can hear Maeve telling tales. I can do this. I'll start right now. Tonight. In the hush of stars, I'll tell Irish tales.

I'll be like Brid. She came all the way across this ocean to take care of her eggs. She didn't care that she'd never see her homeland again. Her nest was her home.

Just as my nest will be. Wherever my child is, that's

where my home is, for this child will give me back my mother tongue, my Eire. How funny; I will live up to my old name of Aist. I'll be as good a parent as any stork.

Breathlessly, I search in the folds of this dress for the secret pockets. It's been so long since I last checked, but, thank the Lord, it's still there: My fingers close around the gold teething ring. Now I have someone to give it to.

From deep within comes the memory of Hoskuld's words as he looked at the ornamented sword back in the north country: *Respect for families is second only to respect for the gods.* Hoskuld has changed, I know he has, despite his brainless words earlier. With this child, he will walk those last few steps toward understanding—for this is his family too.

My son will be a free man. And someday he can travel back to Eire and find out what became of Father, Mother, Nuada. He can go to the land of the *Dubhgall* and learn what became of Brigid. He can soothe my soul at last.

I rub salt on my teeth and rinse my mouth and face. I run my fingers through my hair. I pick at dirty spots on my dress, and smooth the wrinkles flat. I stand up and face the wind blowing off the good land.

AUTHOR'S NOTE

In the Icelandic Saga of the People of Laxardal there is mention of a woman named Melkorka. The chieftain Hoskuld buys her from a Russian slave merchant when he is back in Scandinavia on a trip to get timber to build a new home in Iceland. Melkorka doesn't talk, and Hoskuld knows nothing of her background.

When he arrives with her in Iceland, his wife forbids him to continue using her as a concubine. So she becomes a regular slave. When her child is two years old, Hoskuld overhears Melkorka speaking Gaelic to the boy. That's when Hoskuld discovers she isn't mute at all. And she finally tells him she was an Irish princess who got taken by a slave trader. That's all we ever learn of her past.

In this story I have created a history for Melkorka that is founded on general facts about life in Ireland, Russia, and Scandinavia in the early 900s, trying to find what she must have feared and hoped through her journeys.

ABOUT THE AUTHOR

Donna Jo Napoli is the acclaimed and award-winning author of many novels—both fantasies and contemporary stories. She won the Golden Kite Award for *Stones in Water* in 1997. Her novel *Zel* was named an American Bookseller Pick of the Lists, a *Publishers Weekly* Best Book, a *Bulletin of the Center for Children's Books* Blue Ribbon, and a *School Library Journal* Best Book. A number of her novels have been selected as ALA Best Books. She is the head of the linguistics department at Swarthmore College in Pennsylvania, where she lives with her husband and their children.